$\mathcal{S}$uddenly I felt someone's hands on my shoulders.

"Are you ready for your initiation, newbies?"

Hayden picked me up by the waist sideways, as if I were a suitcase under his arm, and dragged me closer to the water.

I found myself being lifted—and the next thing I knew I was underwater. It was freezing cold and bubbling up all around me as a wave tumbled over my head. My feet were standing on sand and crushed shells.

I surfaced and slicked back my hair, the salt water stinging my eyes.

Hayden was smiling at me as I strode out of the surf. "You actually *liked* that, didn't you?"

I pulled a piece of seaweed off my leg and threw it at him as I walked past. "Doesn't everyone like swimming?" I asked him with a smile.

Also by CATHERINE CLARK
Icing on the Lake
The Alison Rules
Maine Squeeze
Frozen Rodeo
Wurst Case Scenario
Truth or Dairy

CATHERINE CLARK

So Inn Love

HARPER TEEN

An Imprint of HarperCollinsPublishers

HarperTeen is an imprint
of HarperCollins Publishers.

www.harperteen.com

Library of Congress Catalog Card Number:
2006933591
ISBN-10: 0-06-113904-1
ISBN-13: 978-0-06-113904-8

Typography by Andrea Vandergrift
❖
First HarperTeen edition, 2007

So Inn Love

Chapter One

"*A*nd you are?"

You've got to be kidding me.

I was the last person to arrive. I hate walking into a room that's already full of people—even if the room is the front lobby of a gorgeous seaside inn on the coast of Rhode Island, where I was lucky enough to be starting a great new summer job.

Being late wasn't the impression I wanted to make on my first day, especially since I'd barely gotten this job to begin with, and had found out only a week before that it was mine.

"Hi. I'm Elizabeth McKenzie," I said to the woman standing in front of me. She had short, reddish hair and a stocky, athletic build. She was wearing khaki pants and a white Tides Inn polo shirt that looked as if it had been ironed. The short sleeves had actual creases. "But please, call me Liza," I said. "Sorry—am I late?"

"Just a minute or two. Miss Crossley." She held out her hand to shake mine, and gave me a quick once-over glance, as if she was deciding whether to approve of me or not. I was relieved that I'd removed that pink streak from my hair *before* I got here—she didn't seem the type to appreciate things like that. Her handshake was so strong, I nearly winced from her grip. "So you're the last-minute hire," Miss Crossley said.

She didn't sound all that happy with the decision, which was funny considering she was the Inn staff manager and she had to be *in* on hiring me, at some level. I wished she hadn't announced that I was "last minute" like that to the room. Everyone kind of looked up and focused their gaze on me, as if there might be something wrong, or suspect, about me.

As if I'd only made the security clearance by the skin of my teeth. As if I were only good enough when there was no other option.

Or at least that's what their faces told me. That I was being snobbed.

Yes, it's a verb. Especially useful around exclusive communities like this one. I actually hadn't known that much about it until three years ago when, because of my mother's job as a professor, we moved to a new town, where Snobs 'R Us was the name of one of the after-school clubs.

Just kidding. But moving right before sophomore year had been a little traumatic for me. Just when I was working my way up from being a lowly freshman, I had to start all over again, and the cliques at my new school didn't make it easy. It was like everyone had lived in the same town forever and I was the sole new person. That wasn't true, but that's how it felt until I made some friends. Now I was wondering if I'd just walked into the same situation here, at my perfect summer job.

One girl flashed me a sympathetic smile, so at least there was that. The room was filled with about forty people, taking up nearly every seat in the large, spacious lobby. It was starting to hit me that I was actually on the Tides Inn staff. I couldn't believe it. Everything had happened so fast, since I got the summons a week ago. My dream job, coming through. I might be late and I might be a little uncomfortable, but at the same time I knew I was lucky to be here.

I finally spotted an empty white wicker chair by the window, so I nodded to Miss Crossley and scooted past her to take a seat.

"Now, we'll do some introductions later on, once you've had a chance to get settled. But the Inn opens for summer season—the only season we have around here—in two days," she said. "That gives us two days to get completely perfect at everything we do. We don't accept less than perfection here at the Tides Inn. Our customers expect it, and we demand it. You've all been hired because of your extreme trustworthiness."

She made it sound as if we were about to go into battle, and we were the elite soldiers. The Green Berets—although I didn't think the Inn's color scheme was green. More like a blue-gray, the color of a whale you might see if you went out far enough in a sailboat. And instead of berets? We'd probably wear floppy bucket hats.

"Now," Miss Crossley went on, "some of you are new to me, some are old friends—" She stopped as the screen door creaked open and slammed shut with a bang.

A tall guy with brown hair, wearing long khaki shorts, flip-flops, and a navy T-shirt ripped at the neck, stepped into the lobby. He glanced behind him at the door, then turned back to Miss Crossley and smiled. He had the kind of smile that made you like him instantly.

"Someone's going to have to fix that before the guests get here," he said.

"Thanks for volunteering, Hayden. Nice you could make it," the manager said. She cleared her throat as she glanced at her watch.

So I wasn't the last one to arrive, after all. Victory! Or at least not total outright failure. I looked at him; his T-shirt said, "Mapleville Academy" on it, a place I'd only vaguely heard of but probably should know about. I thought it was one of those elite private schools in New England.

"Sorry, Peach. I got lost," he said.

"Peach?" several people repeated.

I'd only met Miss Crossley a minute ago,

but I didn't get the impression that she was very "peachy" at all. Apple, maybe. Granny Smith Apple. Sour.

"In case the rest of you are wondering, Hayden's the only one allowed to call me that." Miss Crossley narrowed her gaze at Hayden. "And even then I'm not so sure, actually. And what do you mean, you got lost? You've been here the past two summers, plus I picked you up from the New York train yesterday. So where have you been?"

"I was trying to clean up the beach. I picked up some bottles and trash, then I was raking the sand—I lost track of time, I guess. Sorry."

"What, are you going for Employee of the Month already?" someone in the crowd called out.

"Hey, if the plaque fits . . . then put it on the wall," Hayden replied with a smile.

The guy sitting behind me groaned.

Miss Crossley didn't look impressed or amused, either. "Hayden, why don't you hurry up and take a seat so we can get started—or restarted, rather."

"Sure thing." He smiled at her.

"There's room here, Hayden." Two girls scooted over on a sofa to make a space for him.

"Now. As I was saying before I was so rudely interrupted . . ." Miss Crossley looked at Hayden and smiled. "It's great to have you all back this year. I know there are other summer jobs that might pay more, might be more exciting, or might be closer to home. We at the Inn — the Talbot family and I, and the rest of the adult employees — certainly appreciate the sacrifices you're making to be here. Living away from home —"

"That's a sacrifice?" the guy sitting behind me on the window seat joked. He was leaning forward onto the back of my chair, and he was sort of pulling my hair. I moved a little to tug it free from under his arm.

"More like a gift," a girl to my left added. I turned to her and smiled in agreement. It wasn't that living at home was so terrible, for any reason — just *old*.

"Well, it's not as if this is the Hilton," Miss Crossley said. "Actually the Inn is better than the

Hilton, of course. But *your* living quarters—"

"More like Motel Six," a girl added.

"No, more like Motel Three," Hayden said, and everyone laughed.

Is it really that bad? I wondered. I mean, I figured that the dorm where all the employees stayed was nothing special, but I thought living on our own was cool enough. We didn't need it to be all that nice, considering we wouldn't be spending a whole lot of time in our rooms.

"Your accommodations are perfectly adequate," Miss Crossley said, the only one who didn't crack a smile. I wondered if she smiled much, period. Probably not. Too busy striving for perfection.

After an hour's worth of rules and regulations, Miss Crossley told us to take a break from orientation and go check out our rooms.

The boy sitting behind me stood and stretched his arms over his head, looking sleepy. "Orientation. Like it's college." He smiled at me. He had curly, sandy hair that he brushed back out of his face. "How much is there to know?"

"A lot, I guess." I didn't want to say anything

bad, seeing as how I was the last person to be hired.

"She thinks so, anyway." He held out his hand. "Hey. I'm Josh."

"Liza," I said. "Nice to meet you."

"So you're new here?" he asked, and I nodded. "Me too. Don't worry, you didn't miss anything by being late," he said. Then he walked over to join and talk to some of the other guys.

I looked around the room at everyone gathered in small groups, talking and laughing and hugging. The way everyone was instantly talking to each other, it was obvious most of them knew each other already, from the summer before.

I glanced down at the information sheets Miss Crossley had handed us when the meeting broke up. "Room Assignments" was on top. I looked around the room at everyone, trying to guess who I might be rooming with, and who might become my good friends—with any luck they'd be the same people. The summer could either be great—which I was desperately hoping for and semicounting on—or terrible, depending.

I was skimming the list for my name when

a petite girl with short dark-brown hair came up to me. She wore a red T-shirt and khaki capri pants. "Hi, I'm Claire. I think you're my roommate," she said.

"Hey!" I said with a smile. "I was just checking out the list and wondering how I'd figure out who you were. You'd think Miss Crossley would make a point of introducing us but . . . Are you psychic?"

"Well, since you came late, I got to hear your name, so I knew it was you," she said. "It wasn't my ESP—sorry."

"I knew there was a reason I came late. Everyone probably thought I was just lazy, or disorganized, but it was all a plan so you'd know who I was. Really."

"Sure. Obviously," Claire said. "I'm the opposite—I always get everywhere early. I even *try* to be late, but it never works out. You think that kind of thing is genetic?"

"I hope so, because that would give me a good excuse for being late," I said.

"Oh, come on. You weren't even the last person to show up. And I think the only person who noticed or cared—"

"Just happens to be our new boss," I put in.

Claire shrugged. "Yeah, so, she'll get over it. It might take her a few weeks, and you might have to be perfect in every other way, but it'll blow over."

"Yeah. Thanks. *That* puts my mind at ease." We both laughed. "Did you work here last summer, too?" I asked Claire. So far she seemed like a really nice person—we'd have no problem getting along. "Because it seems like everyone besides me has."

Claire shook her head. "Oh, I've never worked here before, either."

"Is it me? Or does it seem like kind of a club?" We stood off to the side, watching the other girls squealing and hugging. They were all standing in a circle, and the only two people not in the circle were me and Claire. I felt totally frozen out, just like when I moved to my new school three years ago. I hoped college wasn't going to be anything like this, because I wasn't sure how many times I could go through it.

"I hate cliques. I got enough of this in high school, you know?" Claire said.

As she was talking, I saw a girl over her shoulder who looked very familiar to me. "Me too. Except . . . wait a second. I *know* her," I said. I hadn't noticed her when I came in, but I suddenly realized—it was Caroline Farlane! We both used to vacation in this town when we were kids. My grandparents rented a cottage just down the road, for two weeks every summer. This would be so cool! She kind of had an "in" already, and so could I, just because I knew her.

"Know who?" Claire asked.

Caroline used to be sort of a tomboy, but now she had shoulder-length straight blond hair, bleached and combed to perfection, and wore a flowered sun dress with high-heeled sandals. "Caroline?" I asked as I approached her. "Is that you?"

She turned toward me and gave me a confused look. "I'm sorry?" she said, fingering the strand of pearls around her neck.

"It's me," I said. "Elizabeth McKenzie."

"Oh, wow. Beth. I didn't even recognize you. Like, at all." She stared at my black tank, long khaki shorts, and black sandals.

"But didn't you hear me say my name when I came in?"

"I didn't see you come in. Zoe and I must have been talking," she said. "We had a ton to catch up on. That's Zoe, we're roommates." She pointed to a tall, pretty girl with similar features to her own.

You've heard of "the beautiful people," right? Well, that was Zoe. She was kind of stunning, actually, like she could model if she chose to.

"Anyway, you look . . . totally different." She implied that it was maybe not in a good way. "Is that a tattoo?" She pointed to a symbol on my arm.

"Not a permanent one. Just a last-night-at-home thing. My friends and I—we all did it."

"Hm. Interesting. Because they're banned, you know. If Miss Crossley sees that, you'll be in trouble."

"Noted," I said as I shifted to put my arm behind my back, in case our supervisor was approaching. "It's temporary. I can wash it off."

"Well, I'd suggest it," Caroline said in a snooty tone.

"Yeah, well, I've changed a little since we last saw each other, I guess." I was probably about half a foot taller, for one thing. She was about twice as preppy. Our outfits couldn't have been more different, which was funny, because we used to be so alike. "And I go by Liza now. This is Claire, my roommate. What room are you in?" I asked, wondering if we'd be neighbors.

"Beth, your hair," she said, ignoring my question—and my nickname change. "Didn't it used to be blond?"

"Sort of," I said. "Anyway, how have you been? Wow. It's so cool that we're both working here. Who would have thought?"

"Actually, this is my *second* summer here," she said. Her voice wasn't necessarily cold, but it wasn't warm either.

"Oh." I nodded. What was I supposed to say—congratulations? She was expecting something, so I said, "So you liked it enough to come back?"

"Are you serious? This is the best place to

work. Ever. How did you get in, anyway?" Caroline asked, as if this were the sort of nightclub where I'd be left standing outside, waiting in line forever.

I was going to tell her how hard it had been, and how I'd applied last year, too, and how my grandfather had pulled a few strings to get me in. But her attitude was bugging me, so I decided not to. "Oh, you know," I said. "It wasn't any big deal."

"Really."

"Really," I said. "So tell me what you've been up to. It's been a long time. I can't wait to catch up. You know what's weird, I haven't been inside here for a couple of years. Wow— I just thought of something. Remember when we got kicked off the tennis court here? Oh my God, that was funny."

"We did not."

"We did, too!" I said. "Remember those cute guys we met on the beach, and we were supposed to meet them here, and then—"

"Well, see you around, Beth," she interrupted me. Then she turned back to the group she'd been talking to when I first walked up, to

Zoe and her other friends.

She's snobbing me, I thought. *Caroline, of all people, is snobbing me.* If she was part of the "in crowd," then maybe I didn't want to be. "It's *Liza*," I said to her back.

"Hey, Liza. And don't mind her, she's not that nice to anyone."

I turned and saw Hayden—the guy who'd arrived right after me—standing beside me. "Seriously?"

He nodded. "Caroline's not exactly the person you send out on the welcome wagon."

"Okay, but here's the thing. Have you ever *seen* a welcome wagon? Like, what's in it?"

"And who pulls it? Horses?" Claire added.

We all laughed, that kind of nervous laughter when you first meet someone.

"So you're Liza. And you are?" Hayden asked.

"Claire. We're new hires," she explained. "You know, apparently the only two new people here?"

"Oh, come on, you're not the *only* new ones," Hayden said. "That guy, Josh, over there . . . and that other guy, what's his name. There're at least five or six of you."

"Someone over there just called us newbies," Claire said. "I hate that phrase, or term, or whatever it is."

"I know," I said. "We can't help it if we didn't work here before."

"So, non-newbies," Hayden said. "Don't get a complex. Hayden Overton. Nice to meet you."

"Same here," I said. At least one person in the so-called in crowd was being nice to us. And as I'd learned from moving, that was really all it took. If one person accepted you or decided you were cool—then everyone would.

"You know what? You want to get out of here?" Hayden said.

"Aren't we supposed to go to the dorm?" Claire asked.

"The dorm can wait. *Believe* me," Hayden said. "Especially since—" He stopped and looked at us for a second.

"Since what?" I wanted to know.

He shook his head. "Never mind. We've got half an hour before we need to meet up with Peach again. Come on, let's hit the water."

I looked at Claire. "I'm all for it. You?"

"Sure," Claire said. "Sounds good."

"You know what—I see someone I've got to say hi to. But I'll be right down, okay?" Hayden told us.

"He seems nice," Claire said as we walked outside onto the Inn's back porch, which stretched almost the entire length of the building. It had tables and chairs for guests, and standing on it, we looked straight out at the Atlantic Ocean.

"Very," I agreed. I stood on the steps for a few seconds, admiring the view. Then I stepped off onto the boardwalk and turned to look back up at the Inn. It was as gorgeous as I remembered. It was four stories tall, with white shutters and weather-beaten-looking blue-gray paint. Every room had two windows, and a few of them had small decks with big Adirondack chairs facing the ocean.

On the street side, there was a circular driveway, wide, welcoming steps, and a small open deck with wrought-iron tables and chairs under generous-size canvas umbrellas. The parking lot was set back a bit from the Inn, so small golf-cart shuttles were used to ferry guests and their belongings from their cars.

I loved the salty ocean smell that hit my nose as soon as I turned onto the road toward the beach. It was the same, every year, from the time I was a toddler until now.

The real reason I'd been late for the meeting was that on the way in, I'd stopped the car to get out and just breathe the salt air. It sounds dumb, I know, and I'd probably never admit it to anyone in the room—especially Miss Crossley, who was too no-nonsense for that sort of thing—but it's a ritual of mine.

It's not as if we lived *so* far from the ocean, but I still didn't get there very much, especially not during the school year. Every summer's first trip to Rhode Island made my nose so happy.

My boyfriend back home had been really upset—no, mad—when I told him I was going away for the summer. He didn't understand, but that was because he'd never been here, never seen how gorgeous it was. Anyway, we were only talking about ten weeks. That whole time he'd be busy working the graveyard shift at his uncle's boat factory, and we wouldn't have seen each other even if I was around, working at my dad's law office.

Anyway, it wasn't that kind of relationship. We went out when it was convenient, and we had a good time together—but I wouldn't die without him. I'd never had that kind of feeling for anyone. I didn't think I was the type of person to die for love, anyway. I wasn't into big drama.

"A private beach? This is incredible," Claire said as we stepped off the wooden boardwalk.

I slipped off my sandals before I jumped off into the warm sand. Since the Inn wasn't open for business yet, the beach was all ours. "I've never been on this part of the beach." I pointed to a public beach across the breakwater. "That's where we used to hang out. See how it's all crowded?"

Claire laughed. "You and Caroline hung out over there? Hard to believe."

"Why?"

"Oh, I don't know. You don't seem like . . . the same kind of people. To be friends, I mean."

"No. Not anymore, I guess."

I heard voices behind us and turned to see that everyone else had the same idea. They were all either walking—or sprinting—down to the ocean's edge like us, ditching their shoes and sticking their toes into the ocean.

"So where are you from?" Claire asked.

"I was born in Iowa. But now we live in Connecticut," I said. "Outside Hartford. How about you?"

"Boston," Claire said.

"Cool," I said. "I've only been there once, but I thought it was great."

While we were talking, I was digging my toes into the sand, watching the water roll over my feet, which were sinking a little deeper with each wave and the undertow that followed. I loved that feeling; it was so relaxing.

Suddenly I felt someone's hands on my shoulders.

"Are you ready for your initiation, newbies?"

I turned around and saw Hayden standing behind me. He squeezed my shoulders. "Initiation?" I asked. What was he talking about? This didn't sound good. And here I'd thought he was being so nice to us. "What's that?"

"It's a rite of passage," a guy named Richard said as he swooped up Claire in his arms, with one quick motion.

"Hey! Miss Crossley never mentioned this," Claire said. "Put me down!" she protested.

"You're not actually going to—" I started to say, as I struggled against Hayden. "You're not serious. You think you can—"

"Yeah, I do." He picked me up by the waist, sideways, as if I were a suitcase under his arm, and dragged me closer to the water.

"Since when is there initiation around here?" Claire demanded.

"Since now!" And Richard lifted her in the air and tossed her into the surf.

Before I could laugh at her, I found myself being lifted over Hayden's head—and the next thing I knew I was underwater. It was freezing cold and bubbling up all around me as a wave tumbled over my head. My feet were standing on sand and crushed shells. I surfaced and slicked back my hair, the salt water stinging my eyes. Around me I could hear a few other people complaining, and Claire was yelling at Richard. All the new people were in the water, including Josh. As he waded out, he looked at me and Claire and said, "So it's us against them, huh?"

"I guess so." I glanced back at shore and saw Hayden watching me.

What he didn't know was that I didn't really care if I got tossed in—I was dying for my first swim in the ocean, anyway. So it didn't have to be in my clothes, but I didn't care. What a great feeling.

I looked at my arm and saw my temporary tattoo dissolving in the choppy salt water, colors streaming off my arm. I felt something tugging at me and found a long thick piece of seaweed—the kelp kind that reminds me of lasagna noodles—wrapped around my right leg.

Hayden was smiling at me as I strode out of

the surf. "You actually *liked* that, didn't you?"

I pulled the seaweed off my leg and threw it at him as I walked past. "Doesn't everyone like swimming?" I asked him with a smile.

Chapter Two

"Why do I get the feeling this room is reserved for the new people?"

Claire and I stood in the doorway of Room 213.

"Thirteen equals unlucky," she said.

"Also unfurnished," I said.

Because our room was right next to the stairway, it had a strange, angled shape, like part of it had been chopped off.

"We get one dresser. Everyone else has two," Claire complained. "Our closet is the size of an old telephone booth."

I wandered around the room. It didn't take long. "And look at this chair. There's one arm missing, and stuffing's poking through."

Our room was at the end of the second-floor hall, near the stairs, and had an L-shape, with our beds near the windows. There was a built-in wooden dresser, a tiny closet, one desk for us to share, and one semicomfortable chair with strange orange upholstery. The walls were bare and painted white, but at least there were pretty sage-green curtains on the windows.

I tried to open the windows, but they were jammed. I pounded on the sides to get them to budge. When I finally got them open, a fresh ocean breeze came into the room. I looked out the window. The dorm was set back behind the Inn, down a path, so the ocean view was blocked, but we did have a nice view of the Inn.

"Well, maybe it's small, but I still don't think it's that bad," I said, turning around.

I didn't plan on spending much time in the room anyway, when there was so much to see and do, being right on the ocean like we were. The room would be a place to crash at night, and that was about it.

"Wait until it gets hot in July," Claire said. "No air conditioning, and we're on the second floor. I bet this place gets as humid as any-thing."

"Yeah, but we'll always have that breeze off the water, right?" I pointed out.

Claire narrowed her eyes. "You like getting thrown into the ocean, you like the smell of salt and fish, you don't care that we have the worst room, and you don't mind humidity. . . . You're one of those glass-half-full kind of peo-ple, aren't you?" she asked.

"Sometimes," I said. "It depends on my mood. I can be really dark when I want to." I smiled at her.

"Good. If you were going to be optimistic about everything, I'd go crazy," Claire said. "My mom is like that and it drives me nuts. She's always saying that thing about how when one door closes, another opens, or a window opens when a door gets slammed, or something." She laughed.

"Well, in this place, if a door gets slammed? I think we'll all hear it, whether or not the win-dow's open," I said. From downstairs you could hear guys shouting to each other, while some-one on our floor was blasting music.

The guys all lived on the first floor, and the girls on the second. I was still kind of surprised my parents finally let me go away to such an unsupervised place. Were they really aware of what I was getting into? A coed dorm? Did they not know, or did they know and not care? Were they just getting me prepared for what I'd encounter in college?

Maybe that was why they'd tried to talk me out of this plan at the beginning, even though my grandparents had supported it. They'd also tried to persuade me to go to an all-women's college. That hadn't worked, either.

"How did you end up here?" I asked Claire as I pulled a suitcase onto the bed. It sagged under the weight, which was pathetic considering it wasn't that heavy a bag. The bed felt suspiciously like a cot, the kind that might be issued by the Red Cross during an emergency. Did everyone in the dorm have thin mattresses, I wondered, or just us?

"I needed to get away for the summer," Claire said. She lifted a stack of perfectly folded T-shirts from her suitcase into the dresser.

"I'll take the two bottom drawers, if you'll take the top two, okay?"

"Sure," I agreed. "You were saying . . . you needed to get away?" That was sort of intriguing, as an opening.

"Oh!" She laughed. "No big scandal—I didn't mean it to sound like that. I just couldn't stand another summer at home. Boredom. You know. Plus my older sister worked here a few summers ago and was always telling me how great it was," she said. "And *she* heard about it from her college roommate, who got her in. When I told her I wanted to apply, she said the most important advice she was going to give me was to beware of hookups."

"Beware of hookers? Really? Around *here*?" I tried to imagine a woman in a feather boa and short shorts, down by the boardwalk to the private beach.

"Hook*ups*," Claire repeated with a laugh.

I laughed, too. "Oh! Well, that's okay, I wasn't really planning any."

"Neither am I," Claire said.

I didn't want to completely rule out seeing

someone over the summer, though. I was only human, and who knew what might happen between me and my probably ex, Mark? If we were really over, then I'd be free to date someone else. I didn't have a clue if I would, but I could. The beach would be the perfect romantic location, that was for sure.

"Anyway, my sister just said that this place can get really small, really fast, if you're not careful," Claire continued.

"Hm. Sort of like high school, then?" I asked with a smile.

"Yeah, exactly. God, I'm glad that's over," Claire said.

I nodded in agreement. I was glad to be moving on—and out—to college, too, but I didn't *hate* high school, not after I'd settled in and made new friends. The way I saw it, high school was a lot like a very trendy haircut. Fun while it lasted.

High school could get boring if you were complacent, if you did the same thing over and over. Same with hair. I preferred coloring mine, streaks of blue or sometimes pink, going platinum once or twice, and now, chestnut auburn brown, when I was naturally a blonde. (And no, I'm not going to beauty school. At least not until I flunk out of college.)

Claire unpacked several books, stacking them on the desk, making a bookshelf by using larger stacks at each end of the desk.

"Wow," I said. "Are all those for fun, or . . . ?"

"Reading ahead for freshman year at Columbia. Plus a few for fun." She pulled out a couple of paperback chick-lit novels and grinned. "Chaucer's okay, but . . ."

"Sometimes not so much," I added.

"Exactly."

"Miss Crossley made it sound like we'll be working all the time. Do you think we'll have time to read? And if we do, can I borrow *that* one? Not the Chaucer."

Outside our window, a bullhorn sounded. "Come on, everyone, time to tour the Tides!" Miss Crossley's voice boomed through a megaphone.

"She's so high energy it's painful. I meant to

wash my hair after the salt swim, but, oh well."
Claire sighed as she grabbed a ball cap from
the desk and pulled it over her head.

"Good idea." I grabbed my Tigers Volleyball cap.

When Claire and I walked outside, Miss
Crossley met us with a look of disapproval. She
was good at doing that. "Dress code rule number seventeen. No ball caps," she said.

There's a dress code? I thought. *Why did no one
tell me?* "Oh. Sorry—" I started to apologize.

"No ball caps, except these." Miss Crossley
opened a large plastic bag and handed us each
an official Tides Inn cotton cap. They were different shades of sun-washed pastel, and the one
I grabbed was a pale orange. I caught Hayden's
eye as I pulled it over my head. He was already
wearing a white one.

"How do you guys like your room?" Caroline asked.

"Fine. Thanks." I smiled at her. "It's very
scenic."

"And spacious, don't forget spacious,"
Claire added.

"What's wrong with your room?" Miss

Crossley asked as we assembled into a group outside the dorm.

"Oh, uh, nothing," I said. "It's fine."

"Good. So, moving on. Today we'll get the big overall picture," Miss Crossley went on. "You all need to understand the complete workings of the Inn. In case you're required to fill in for anyone, you should know a little about each other's jobs."

"Miss Crossley, do we really need to do this again? I mean, some of us were here last year, we know the drill," Zoe said. "How about if we split up and—"

"Zoe, you know as well as I do that a refresher course is never a bad idea," Miss Crossley interrupted.

Zoe didn't look as if she knew that at all. She turned to Caroline and rolled her eyes. The two of them definitely acted as if they were too good to be bothered.

"Now, you guys should know the rules. Day One, we stick together. That's our philosophy. Teamwork. Day Two, you focus on your particular area of responsibility."

"Day Three, we run away," Josh muttered,

beside me. Since he was new, I wondered if he had an equally crappy room on the first floor, beneath us.

"Day Three, we hit the beach, right?" another person added.

"Only if your job is lifeguarding," Miss Crossley said sternly.

"No problem," Hayden said.

So that was why he'd been cleaning up the beach. It was his turf.

It figured that he was a lifeguard, I thought. He had the body for it. He'd lifted me like I weighed nothing, plus he had broad shoulders, plus he had the kind of rock-hard abs people refer to as a six pack . . .

Hey. I'm just reporting what I saw when he picked me up to toss me into the surf, okay? Strictly a journalistic effort.

"Listen up!" Miss Crossley said, interrupting my happy memory. "Here is the most important area of the entire Inn. The entrance. What guests see here influences their entire stay with us."

"So in other words, no hanging out by the

entrance, smoking?" Hayden joked.

"No smoking anywhere on hotel grounds," Miss Crossley said. "Unless of course a guest requests that you step outside and offers you a cigar—"

"Then we *have* to smoke?" Claire interrupted.

"No, I was only joking. Though you should make sure he or she has a light!" Miss Crossley smiled.

"All right, Peach. Loosening up," Hayden said.

"Don't count on it," she replied sternly.

"Lighting cigars for people? My sister didn't mention the part about indentured servitude," Claire said quietly to me as we all moved into the Inn.

"I'm guessing there's a lot she left out," I whispered back.

Once inside, I checked out the reception and lobby area—when I'd come through earlier, I'd been in such a rush that it had all been a blur. There were sofas, big, comfy dark-brown leather ones, wicker ones for those in wet swimsuits, tables with issues of current magazines, and bookshelves from which guests could borrow any book they wanted. The reception desk was made of a rich, dark wood. Behind it were mailboxes for the rooms. An old-fashioned silver bell sat on the desk, beside the fountain pen guests would use to sign the Inn's register. It was like something out of an old movie.

We used to come to the Inn's restaurant for lunch when my grandparents rented a small cottage down the road. Only once a summer, though, because it was too pricey, according to my grandmother, who, to be fair, could cook up a lobster and clam dinner herself that was equally good, if not better.

Still, I used to look at the teen servers and wish I could work here, especially a couple of years ago when I was desperate for a summer job. I always wanted to stay here, too, but my parents pointed out that not only was it too expensive, it would be silly considering my grandparents rented a cottage so close by.

Now I was going to be working here, at the front desk. Life was so weird sometimes. I was grateful to whoever had dropped out of the staff to make room for me. "Claire, did I tell you? This is where I'm going to be," I started to tell her.

"Actually, Elizabeth, I need to talk to you about that," Miss Crossley interrupted me.

Liza, I wanted to say, but didn't. "You do?"

"Yes. There have been some reassignments."

"There have?" I asked.

"Yes. Even though you were hired to help in the guest reception area, we've decided to go with someone with more experience," Miss Crossley explained. "Caroline pointed out that she has been here longer, and that it is a job she's wanted all along. So we reassigned you, based on seniority."

Or lack thereof, I thought as I checked out the area where I wouldn't be sitting, wouldn't be answering the phone, and wouldn't be greeting celebrities and other interesting people as they arrived.

Caroline looked at me and smiled. "It takes someone who knows the Inn inside and out. I'm *really* sorry, Beth," she said, in a voice so obviously phony that I knew she wasn't sorry at all. And if she knew the Inn so well, why hadn't she been the one who got the job in the first place?

"It's Liza," I reminded her. "And that's okay," I said, smiling at her. "I'm sure any job here is great, no matter what it is. So, what do you have for me then?" I asked Miss Crossley cheerfully. Stiff upper lip, glass half full, and all.

"Housekeeping," she said.

My heart sank. I was in trouble. They really hadn't read my application, had they? "Housekeeping" was ranked last on my list of desired positions. I was really terrible about cleaning my room at home. They should have asked my parents for references, because when it came to keeping a place neat and tidy? I had zero skills.

"Housekeeping," I repeated slowly. "Well, okay. I can keep house with the best of them," I lied.

"Happy to hear that," Miss Crossley said. "This is a team effort, and we need team players."

Okay, I thought. *But do I have to be on the clean team?*

I glanced at Caroline, who was smiling happily at her friend Zoe. Caroline had just gotten upgraded from housekeeping to front desk; of course she was happy. But I had a feeling that any idea I had that Caroline and I might still be able to be friends was as dead in the water as my front-desk job.

It's us against them, Josh had said. Was it really going to be that bad?

I was back in my room, tucking the sheets under my thin mattress, when Claire walked in carrying a couple of sodas. "You're not practicing, are you?" she asked.

I sank onto the bed with a sigh. "I know you don't want to hear this, as my roommate, but I'm not the neatest person. Having a job where I'm supposed to clean up after people is like . . . completely against type." Miss Crossley had given me a ten-minute seminar on "Ways to Remove Sand from a Carpet" that I'd already forgotten. Or blocked out. One of the two.

Claire handed me a soda. "You want to switch? I'll clean, you take kids sailing?"

"I don't know how to sail," I said. "Not well enough to teach it, anyway. I mean, if I were stranded on a desert island and sailing was the only way to get off, I suppose I'd figure it out, but . . ."

"I'll teach you," she offered.

"You're crazy. You're going to trade being outside on the water all day with inhaling harmful cleaning products?"

"You can always open the windows to let the fresh air in. You know, your famous ocean breeze," she reminded me.

I frowned at her. "Thanks."

"Besides, didn't she say they only use environmentally safe products that are organically made?" Claire asked.

"Okay, fine, whatever. Organic or not, it's still strong-smelling stuff to cover other, less pleasant stuff, isn't it?" I laid back on the bed and groaned.

Claire collapsed on her bed, laughing. "I'm not laughing *at* you. I'm laughing *with* you. Really."

There was a loud, booming knock on our door. I sat up and was surprised to see several guys crowded into our doorway: Tyler, Hayden, Richard, Daunte, and a few others whose names I hadn't yet memorized.

"So. You're the ones with Room Two-thirteen." Daunte nodded. "All right."

"'All right' what?" Claire asked.

"You should keep it down," Richard said. "There's a noise limit."

"There is?" I asked. Apparently there were lots of rules about this place I hadn't been clued in to yet. Was I missing all the handouts, or what?

"Yeah. If you want to be really loud, you have to come down to the beach with us," Tyler said. "We all go to Crandall's to kick off the summer."

"It's tradition. You have to come," Hayden said.

"Have to," Claire repeated, not sounding convinced. "Or . . . ?"

"You know what happened earlier?" Richard asked her. "Cold seawater, up your nose? More of that."

"Are you even supposed to be up here?" Claire asked. "I thought there were some fairly specific rules about 'fraternizing.' In other words, don't."

"Don't tell me you guys are follow-the-rules

types," Hayden said.

"Not always," I said. "But on our first night? Kind of. Especially since we're new here, and people seem to love giving us a hard time about that."

"We'd never do that," Hayden said. "Us?"

"No, of course not," I said. "And we'd never throw seaweed at you."

He smiled at me.

Caroline pushed her way through the crowd. "If they don't want to come, don't make them," she said. "Maybe they just want to hang out here."

For some reason, that settled the matter for me. "Hang out here? In the dreaded Two-thirteen? I don't think so. Come on, Claire. Let's go."

"But—"

"It'll be fun," I said. "Grab a sweater."

"So this is Crandall's Point. Who or what is a Crandall?" Josh asked.

"It's the huge place up there, the one you can see from here." Caroline pointed to a gigantic, secluded house that looked almost as big as the Inn. "It belongs to the Crandall family and has for years. They made tons of money in the shipping business. You know, back when it was with actual ships. The eighteen hundreds."

She was acting like such a know-it-all that it really bothered me.

"Legend has it that Captain Crandall was out at sea, and he was several weeks late getting home. His wife used to pace back and forth on the widow's walk up there, looking for him and waiting, and she actually fell off—or jumped, some people say. He came home safely, but she was dead," I said.

"What? How did you know that?" Hayden looked at me, impressed.

"I used to come here with my grandparents. Way back when." *When Caroline wasn't so annoying.*

"I'll never look at the house the same way again," Richard said. "I had thought it was a bunch of old money, but now it's a lot creepier."

I thought of the time Caroline and I had met a Crandall cousin when we were taking a kayak class offered by the yacht club. Afterward we'd decided to go visit him, so we'd gone up to the Crandalls' house, rung the doorbell, and then ran away when we chickened out. I think a butler came to the door. I'm not sure, because my view had been blocked by the hedge I'd hid behind.

I wondered if Caroline remembered that, too.

"But they don't own this part, do they?" another new girl named Brooke asked.

"Own the sand and rocks?" Caroline scoffed. "No, I don't think so. I mean, they're not *that* rich."

"So how does the Inn get away with having a private beach, then? They must own it, too, right?" Josh asked.

"Some ancient law preserves their right to it, I think," Hayden said. "They don't own it, exactly, but no one else can use it. Go figure."

"So, can these Crandall people see us down here?" Claire asked.

"No. Well, if they can, they don't care we're here," Zoe said. "At least they've never said anything before."

"Having said that, I wouldn't run around

naked or anything," Hayden suggested. "Just to play it safe."

"Oh, good, I'm glad you warned me, I was just about to do that." Claire rolled her eyes. "You know, you can take them out of high school, but can you take high school out of them?" she asked, and all of the girls laughed.

"Yes, but it's a painful procedure," Zoe said, and we laughed again.

Some of the other guys walked up carrying pieces of driftwood they'd collected. They dropped them into a fire ring made of stones and arranged them for lighting.

"Are we supposed to have fires here?" Claire asked as Richard struck a few matches and tried to get the fire going.

"We always do. It's fine," Hayden said.

"Fine, as in allowed? Or fine, as in you've never gotten caught?" Claire asked.

"We never got in trouble *last* summer," Caroline said.

"Obviously people can see us out here, so if it was a big problem, they'd tell us." Hayden shrugged. "We don't cause any trouble around town, so it's no problem."

"You know what? I still think I'm going to take off," Claire said to me in a soft tone.

"Are you seriously worried? They wouldn't fire us. The Inn opens tomorrow, they need us," I said.

"Who needs us?" Josh asked as he crouched in the sand beside me.

"Miss Crossley, the Talbot family, you know—everyone," I said.

"They do need us, but you should know—they're not afraid of canning employees," Zoe said. "Last summer they fired a couple of people."

"Oh yeah," Caroline said. "What was her name, the one with the tattoo . . . ?" She looked meaningfully at me, and I held up my arm to show her it had washed off. She ignored me.

"Terri," someone else added.

"Right. And what about that guy who partied with the guests after a wedding, and they found him sleeping on the front porch?" Caroline said. "Theo. Remember?"

"Miss Crossley went on a lecture for like a

day and a half about how wrong *that* was," Zoe told us.

"Okay. That's all I need to hear," Claire said, standing up and brushing the sand off the back of her shorts.

"Come on, relax. We're not doing anything illegal," Hayden said. "It's a bonfire. People build them on the beach all the time."

"Yeah, but . . . wasn't there something in our handouts about no beach parties?"

"What are all these handouts everyone keeps talking about? Why didn't I get them?" I asked.

"I don't know, but I have them all back at the room," Claire said.

"Miss Crossley would love to give you your own copies, too," Tyler said. "She can probably quote them from memory."

"Anyway, technically this isn't a beach party. It's a gathering," Daunte said. "Stick around."

Despite everyone's protests, Claire took off to go back to the dorm along with a few others, while the rest of us sat around the bonfire.

"Okay, so you guys have to give us the dirt.

The skinny. The four one one," I said.

"What on earth are you talking about?" Caroline said. Why did everything she said to me end up sounding so disapproving? She sounded like a very uptight librarian at a very uptight library.

"You know, could you please give us the benefit of your venerable experience?" I turned to Caroline. "Is that better?"

A few of the guys laughed, including Hayden, and so did Zoe.

"Tell us what we need to know so we don't screw up," Josh said.

I nodded. "Nice translation. Thanks. Most of you guys have been here before, so tell us about it." I took a handful of sand and let it run through my fingers.

"Okay, well, here's what I would say." Zoe lifted a chunk of her long, straight dark-brown hair and flipped it over her shoulder. "You want to get on Mr. Talbot's good side, as soon as you can."

"Oh yeah. If you can do that, you're golden," Hayden put in.

"Is it hard?" I asked.

"And which Mr. Talbot?"

"Yeah, aren't there two of them? At least?"

"There's the younger one, who's not that young—he's like forty-five—and then there's the older one, who's seventy," Zoe said.

That was the one my grandfather knew. He called him "Bucko," but his name was actually William.

"The younger one goes by William, the older by Bill," another guy explained. "Not to us, though, of course."

"Isn't there a Mr. Talbot the third, too?" Josh asked.

"Yeah, Will, but he's only five," Hayden said. "So you don't need to worry, unless of course you end up having him in your play-group one day. Who's got the little tykes group this summer?"

A couple of girls raised their hands.

"I hear he's kind of a brat. Is that true?" one of the girls asked.

"He's not bad. At least he wasn't last year."

"Anyway. How do we get the adult Talbots to like us?" I asked. I hoped I might have a head start, since my grandfather knew

Mr. Talbot Senior. Still, it had taken me two years to get hired, despite that. Hopefully Mr. Talbot Senior hadn't soured on Grandpa, for some unknown reason. Hopefully Grandpa had been keeping up with his calls and Christmas cards and old-boy network stuff, like sharing jokes and cigars now and then. Virtually. Via e-mail.

"It's easy," Hayden said. "Just flatter them."

"Yeah, but not in a phony way," Zoe said. "They're really nice guys, actually. Whatever happens, they're just trying to protect the Inn's image, so every once in a while, they flip out over something small," she explained.

"Like what?" I asked.

"You'll just have to find out on your own," Caroline said, in a somewhat ominous tone, as if I were bound to screw up. I got the impression that if I were drowning, she wouldn't throw me a life preserver. I don't even think she'd try. She'd probably turn and walk the other way.

What had I done? Was I forgetting some major slight on my part? Or was she remembering one that never happened?

I usually find a way to get along with almost everyone. The real person to worry about wasn't going to be a Talbot. It was *her*.

"Okay, so you asked us what you need to know about the Inn," Hayden said. "So tell us what we need to know about you." He looked right at me.

"Me?" I asked. "Don't start with me."

He laughed. "Why not?"

"I don't know. I'm not that interesting," I said. That wasn't it, but I just didn't feel like talking about myself to a bunch of people I didn't know. "I'd rather hear about stuff from you guys."

"'Not that interesting,'" Josh repeated. "Hm. You know, the people who say stuff like that are always the *most* interesting."

"You know, that's true." Hayden smiled at me across the bonfire.

Why were they ganging up on me? "What can I tell you? I'm from a suburb outside Hartford, I'm cocaptain of the volleyball team, my birthday's March twelfth, which means I'm a Pisces. Oh and I also like piña coladas and walks in the rain," I said. "That's about it."

"Righhhht," Hayden said slowly.

"Okay, you're right, you really *aren't* interesting," Caroline declared.

"Fine, then." I turned to her. "Why don't *you* talk about yourself?" She probably liked to do that.

"We could be here for hours," Daunte joked.

"Stop it." Caroline laughed and tossed a handful of sand in his direction.

"Not cool. Not cool. I have contacts, remember?" Daunte rubbed at his eyes.

"You know, we could sit here all night trading astrological signs. But I think I'd rather go swimming. Anyone else?" I asked.

"Race you," Hayden said as he jumped to his feet.

"No fair — I don't know the way —"

"The ocean? It's right over there," Tyler said.

"I know, but —"

"Last one in is a rotten quahog!" Hayden yelled.

"Ew. Smelly," Caroline was commenting as I took off running for the water, stepping over rocks and stripping off my clothes as I did.

Don't worry, it wasn't *that* racy—I was wearing a bathing suit underneath.

I was tiptoeing into my room later that night when I knocked a book off the edge of the desk. It crashed to the floor and I saw Claire turn over in bed. "Sorry—I was trying not to wake you up so I didn't want to turn on the light," I said.

"It's okay. I heard you guys coming a mile away."

"Really?" I asked.

"Oh yeah. Remember not to say anything personal as you're walking up the path—you can hear everything," Claire said. "So how was it? Sounded like fun."

"It was great. A bunch of us went swimming, which was so cool, but kind of scary, too—I've hardly ever gone swimming at night in the ocean."

"It's dangerous," Claire mumbled into her pillow.

"Yeah, but Hayden was there, plus Lindsay, who lifeguards at the pool, plus Sara, who teaches swimming," I told her. "So I figured I was safe, but you're right, it is kind of weird only using the light of the moon to see by. The water was calm, though. Anyway, half of us were swimming, the other half were watching out for us. It took me forever to find my clothes afterward—never leave your clothes on the beach when it's dark."

I kept babbling for a few more minutes before I realized Claire had gone back to sleep.

I quickly changed into my pajamas and climbed into bed. I guess I should have showered, because my skin was sticky with salt, but I didn't care. It would get old after a few weeks, but for now it was perfect, unlike the rock-hard cot I was lying on top of. Maybe I'd be more comfortable sleeping on the sandy beach, under the stars, I thought as I snuggled under the covers.

I thought of the way Hayden had looked at me as we both sprinted into the ocean, racing each other to be first to dive in. Afterward we'd all sat around the bonfire to warm up and dry off, and I'd caught him looking at me a few times across the fire.

So what? So you're kind of—or more than kind of—attracted to him, I thought as I tried to fall asleep. *You're not here to fall in love over the summer. That would only make everything really complicated.*

You're here to save money for college, and just have fun, I reminded myself.

But . . . wouldn't being in love *be* fun?

Chapter Three

Vacuuming. I hate vacuuming.

I ran the heavy industrial vacuum around the room, starting near the window and working my way backward to the bed. This was my fifth guest room so far, and I was cruising, nearly done with my block of rooms. I'd been lucky and nothing too challenging (or disgusting) had come up yet.

Although there was one challenge: The vacuum had superstrong sucking power and would sort of take off on its own if you didn't keep a tight grip on the handle. I could totally picture it taking off down the hall, cleaning everything in its path—and knocking down a few people, too. It seemed sort of possessed, like something you'd encounter in a horror novel. The fact that Mr. Knight, the "Clean Team" supervisor, had *named* all the vacuums, and this one was the "Hulk," worried me.

Mr. Knight had spent a few hours with us the day before, going over procedures, like how we could use special sticky tape to lift sand out of hard-to-clean places. He'd tested us by making rooms dirty and then having us clean them. He literally had white gloves he used to test our "surfaces," as he called them.

My test went something like this:

Mr. Knight: "And would you say that this is clean?"

Me: "Ye-es."

Him: "You call this clean."

Me: "Yes."

Him: "Really."

And then he showed me the white glove, which was not so white.

"So this is what they mean by commercial strength," I mumbled now as I kept vacuuming. I was being extra thorough, as instructed, so I pushed the vacuum underneath the bed and moved it around searching for "Inn bunnies," as Mr. Knight called them. Suddenly I heard a loud whirring sound. *Uh oh,* I thought, quickly shutting off the vacuum. Had it eaten the bedspread?

I pulled the Hulk toward me, but the wheels wouldn't roll—they were jammed. And then I smelled something burning.

I quickly unplugged the vacuum and laid it on the floor. A black belt was wrapped around the roller on the bottom—and I didn't think it was part of the vacuum. I got down on my hands and knees and started to tug on the belt. Suddenly I saw a pair of feet in shiny black loafers standing beside the vacuum.

I looked up with a feeling of dread.

"What is going on here?" Mr. Knight demanded. "Have you broken the Hulk?"

"What? Come on, no one can bring down the Hulk," I joked.

"What have you done, Liza? It smells like you slipped a belt," he said.

"Something like that." Slipped one, devoured another. No steps forward, two steps back. I tugged at the belt that had gotten sucked into the vacuum, but no matter how hard I pulled,

I couldn't get it free.

"Let me see that." Mr. Knight crouched beside me and examined the vacuum's rollers. "You've ruined it," he said sadly. "I think you've ruined it."

"Wait," I said. "Maybe if we both pull really hard—"

"No, this requires a professional. Leave it." He stood up and brushed the dust off his knees. I reluctantly got to my feet, too. "I'll need to fix up the vacuum before we can get anything else done here. You're excused, for now."

"Excused?" I asked. That didn't sound good, at all.

"Free to go. Take a walk. I'll contact you later about making up the lost time," Mr. Knight said. "You can work a double shift tomorrow."

"Great. Sounds great," I said, faking a smile. *And after that, I'll do a triple shift, and then a quadruple shift* . . . But as much as I hated cleaning, I'd do anything he asked in order to stick around and make up for my mistake. "And I'm *really* sorry about the Hulk. And the belt."

"What belt?"

I turned around and saw a man in tennis whites, holding a couple of racquets, in the doorway.

Time to make my escape, I thought as I edged toward the doorway. "I'm sorry, sir. I didn't realize your belt was under the bed, and the vacuum didn't either until it was too late —"

"You ruined my *belt*? My Etienne Lavager belt? Do you know how much those cost?" the guest demanded.

"It may not be ruined," Mr. Knight said. "Just one moment." Finally he managed to unhook the belt from the vacuum roller, and it whipped through the air as it came free, snapping against the bedpost. When he held it up, there was a big crease in the middle and the edges were frayed.

Mr. Knight cleared his throat. "Of course, the Inn will reimburse you for the belt."

"You don't understand. That's the only belt I have *with* me."

Great. Now I was responsible for this guy's pants falling down, too.

"I'll need a replacement. Or twice the replacement value," the guest demanded.

"Certainly, sir, certainly." While Mr. Knight scrambled to make things right, I hurriedly ducked out into the hallway. I walked down the hall to the stairway at the end as quickly as I could. If this guy ever got his belt back, he'd probably try to strangle me with it.

So, Day One on the job had been a bit problematic. But in my defense? I'd told them not to put me in housekeeping! This sort of thing wouldn't happen at the front desk, I thought as I walked through the lobby, where Caroline was busy chatting with a couple of guests. I would be great at her job—and I wouldn't be at risk of getting fired. Though I couldn't exactly say this was all Caroline's fault, I wanted to, anyway.

I was almost out the door when I heard sandals skittering on the floor behind me. "Beth, where are you going?"

I turned around. Caroline was hurrying up to me. "Is everything *okay*? You look upset. Aren't you supposed to still be working?"

I looked at her for a second. I could tell her everything that had just happened. That was clearly what she wanted me to do, for some reason. We could laugh about it, or maybe I'd end up crying. But she was the last person I wanted to tell about my rocky start at the Inn. I had a feeling she'd enjoy it too much. "Everything's just fine," I said. "I finished early." Then I smiled, because that wasn't a lie—just a different take on things. "See you later!"

I grabbed my iPod and headed out for a walk along the winding oceanfront road. I took my time, admiring the beautiful large homes that faced the sea. I just tried to enjoy breathing in the salt air, while I calmed down by listening to loud music.

I could give up, go home, get back together with Mark. . . . I could do the same old thing I did last summer. But that wasn't me. I didn't quit things. Definitely not after one day. When I was second team on the volleyball team, I worked my way up to captain. When I bombed my SATs on the first take, I took them again and again.

After walking for a while, I came around a curve and saw fellow newbie Josh, walking from the other direction. He had a small brown bag from the candy shop in one hand and a can of energy drink in the other.

"You know it's a wealthy little town when the only shopping options are seafood, candy, and crafts," he said when we got closer. He brushed his sandy-brown hair out of his eyes.

"Postcards everywhere. Food? Not so much," I said. "Right?"

"Yeah, I was hoping for a burger and fries, but I guess you have to have a car for that." He held up the small bag. "I've got Smarties and Laffy Taffy, though."

I laughed. "Those should hold you over until dinner. So how was the job this morning?"

"Brainless. I made a few mistakes, but nothing major."

"Hm. Wish I could say the same." I explained about the housekeeping disaster, how I had mangled a belt and brought down the Inn's most cherished vacuum. "They'll probably ask me to leave, so I figured I should walk around and enjoy the scenery before I go."

"Leave? You're not going to *leave*." Josh

rolled his eyes. "Mistakes happen, right? Like this morning, when I brought the wrong order to the table where the younger Mr. Talbot was sitting with this guy who turned out to be president of the country club. They had a cow. But no, I'm not getting fired. Actually they didn't even complain all that much, just made a bunch of comments about squeaky wheels on opening day."

"Well, I must have been the squeakiest. Or maybe the smelliest. The vacuum practically started smoking."

"Doesn't it know that's harmful to its health?" Josh asked, and I laughed. "And you — you were exposed to secondhand vacuum smoke, so you can sue the hotel if they try to get rid of you. Anyway, where are you going? Postcards or candy?"

"Just for a walk. Visiting my old favorite places from when my family used to vacation here," I said. I debated whether to tell him where I was headed, but decided to keep it to myself, for now. I kind of felt like I needed some more time by myself.

"So, is it turning into one of those you-can't-go-home-again experiences?" Josh asked.

"Not yet. Anyway, see you around. Enjoy that candy."

Actually there was an off-the-main-road little coffee shop called Sally's Tea Room that I knew about. Maybe it was mean of me, but I didn't want to tell Josh and spoil it—not yet. I figured the place could be my escape, if it was still around—I hadn't been here the summer before, and I was hoping it hadn't vanished.

It was located inside an old, vacated bait shop, and the tiny sign by the door didn't give much away. Sally used to say she didn't want any tourists—just locals who got close enough to see that little NO MORE BAIT—JUST COFFEE sign.

I opened the door and went inside. Sally was still there, behind the counter, and the place was lively—all six tables were full. I said hello to her and ordered a large coffee. When I turned around from putting milk in my cup, I nearly dropped it on my feet.

Hayden was sitting at one of the tables. He

wore deep orange-red lifeguard shorts and a white tee, and he was reading a book. "Hey, new girl," he said when he saw me.

"El—"

"Elizabeth. I know." He smiled. "Actually it's Liza. Have a seat." He pushed out the empty chair opposite him with his foot.

I smiled.

"You can call me Hayden," he said. "In case you forgot."

I hadn't.

"But not 'Hay' for short. It's a little too barn-friendly," he said.

"Besides, then people would say things like 'Hey, Hay,' which would be annoying," I pointed out.

"That's already happened. Way too many times." Hayden rolled his eyes. "So don't start, okay?"

I pointed to the paperback thriller he was reading. "I read that a couple weeks ago. It's good, don't you think?"

"Yeah, I kind of can't put it down. That's why I escaped here to read on my lunch break.

Do you read a lot?"

"Tons," I said. "But not as much as Claire, I don't think — you should see how many books she brought."

"Good, I'll know where to go to borrow some then," Hayden said.

I smiled, thinking of the chick-lit novels Claire had unpacked. It was weird. A bunch of people *were* snobby, but Hayden didn't appear to be, which was cool considering he could be. He was the one who'd worked at the Inn three summers straight, and he seemed to sort of call the shots around the place.

"How did you know about this place?" he asked.

"My family used to vacation here, remember?" I said. "Why, did you think you discovered it?"

He laughed. "Kind of. This is my hideout. Not that I need to hide. I'm just saying, I come here to get away from the Inn. To read. Anyway, how's it going?"

"That depends." I took a sip of coffee. I knew I should be having herbal tea, to soothe my frazzled nerves, but that just isn't like me. Once I get totally frazzled, I tend to like to stay that way. Being mellow and laid-back is over-rated, anyway. "Is getting talked to by the house-keeping supervisor on your first day a good thing?"

"Oh no. Tell me you're not working for Uptight Knight," Hayden said.

"Perfect nickname," I murmured. "And I don't know if I'm still working for him."

"Did you know he's in the family?" Hayden said.

"He is? You mean, in the Inn family?" I asked. "Is that redundant?"

He laughed. "Yeah, he's some Talbot cousin or other. He's not Mr. Talbot Junior's first cousin, I don't think, maybe he's one of those twice-removed-type deals."

I sighed. "Great. I think I'm about to be twice-removed, then." Was it too soon to call my grandfather and ask him to put in *another* good word for me?

"No, don't worry, nobody likes him," Hayden said.

"Good," I sighed.

"Not even Mr. Talbot Senior," Hayden added. "Supposedly he had to give him a job because he was in the family, so they stuck him with housekeeping."

I raised my eyebrow. "Is that where they put all the people they don't like?"

Hayden laughed. "No! Well, at least I don't think so. I don't know."

"Great. Thanks. So you're the lifeguard?" I asked.

"One of them," he said. "Plus I drive the Inn shuttle van, usually in the evening, unless something different comes up. You know, we pick up guests at the train station. There's a train that gets in around seven—at least it's supposed to—from New York, and one from Boston that gets in slightly later."

"I love taking the train," I said.

"Oh yeah, me, too," Hayden said. "That's how I got here. See—" Hayden's cell phone rang, and he pushed his chair back from the table. "Sorry. I'll see you around, okay?" Then he went outside to take the call, which I have to say was kind of rude and kind of polite at the same time.

We were under strict orders never to use phones while we were on duty, not even to check our voice mail or e-mail. They were strictly for downtime, which meant I was planning to call my friends at home during my breaks and lunch hour. I took my phone out of my pocket and just as I did, it started to ring. I didn't recognize the number on my caller ID, but I picked up anyway.

"Hey, Liza? Miss Crossley was just here looking for you," Claire said.

I nearly choked on my coffee. "You're kidding."

"No. She wants to talk to you about something. I'm really sorry, but I gave her your number—I had to!"

"It's okay. Hey, how was sailing?"

"There were like ten kids for one boat. I'm just hanging out in our room for a couple of minutes recovering before my afternoon session." She paused. "In comparison to your job, not so bad, I guess. How was scrubbing toilets?"

I laughed. "That went okay, but then I

trashed the vacuum cleaner." My phone started to beep, as another call came in. "I'll explain later—see you!"

"Is this Liza McKenzie?" Miss Crossley asked when I answered. "Where are you?"

"I'm on my lunch break." I supposed you could call it that. "In fact, I was just talking to Hayden. He's here on his break, too." I figured dropping his name couldn't hurt.

"Where is *here*, Liza? I need to talk to you now." Miss Crossley clearly was not impressed. "Could you meet me in my office in five minutes?"

"I don't think I can get there that fast. How about in fifteen?" I suggested, feeling very nervous. Had Mr. Knight gone to find her after he'd yelled at me? Was I going to be fired already?

Remember what Josh said, I told myself. They're not going to fire you. They won't. They can't. Not so close to the start of the season.

Of course, I'd been hired off the waiting list. Which meant there was probably *still* a waiting list.

"Ten minutes, Liza," Miss Crossley said.

I guessed that was her idea of compromising. "That's great!" I said.

How many times was I going to be phony and say that today? I was getting kind of unimpressed with myself.

I tossed my cup into the trash, waved goodbye to Sally, and hurried outside. To my surprise, Hayden was standing there. He was closing his phone with a snap, and about to climb on a bicycle. He looked around as I came out the door.

"Can I borrow that?" I asked, pointing to his bike. "Miss Crossley's kind of breathing down my neck—or cell phone anyway—she wants me there in ten minutes and I don't think I can run that fast."

"I have a better idea," Hayden said. "Why don't we both ride?"

"How are we going to do that?"

"Easy. I pedal, you sit on the handlebars."

"You sure that will work? I'm kind of tall," I said.

"Well, you could sit on the seat and I could stand and pedal," Hayden suggested.

I eyed the bike, which was a cruiser style with fat tires. "Where did you get this, anyway?" I asked.

"Oh, there's a shed out behind the Inn. It's got tons of old stuff like this. They used to be for nice bike rentals but they're really old."

"And anyone can use them?" I asked.

"Sure. You just need a key to the shed." He smiled and held up a small key. There was a semiarrogant tone that went with that, but I didn't mind. He had a bike—I needed one. "Climb on," he said.

I walked around to the front of the bike. "I haven't tried this since I was about six. I was a lot shorter then."

"And lighter, probably," Hayden said, adjusting his stance a little as we prepared to set off.

Was he trying to imply something? "Hey. If you want, I can pedal and you can ride." I looked over my shoulder at him as I balanced myself on the handlebars.

"I was kidding, okay? And you're only offering that because you just realized that if we crash, you'll go down first," Hayden said.

"I hadn't even gotten to thinking about crashing yet." As Hayden pushed off, I squealed and lifted my feet, and we started to wobble along the street. Fortunately there wasn't much traffic, which was good because we were weaving all over the place until Hayden straightened out the bike.

"You doing okay?" Hayden called up to me.

"This is great—" I started to say, honestly this time.

Then we hit a giant pothole.

The bike tilted to the right, jolting me off the handlebars. I landed on my feet, just as Hayden hopped off the bike, grabbing me by the waist to steady me. I looked over my shoulder at him. "I'm okay," I said.

"Sorry. I thought you were—uh—falling." He looked very embarrassed, which was kind of an odd look for him.

"No. I'm fine," I said.

Hayden leaned down to pick up the bike, while I refastened the elastic in my hair, which had come loose in all the excitement of the near-crash. "Maybe I should just walk," I said. "If I run, I could—"

"It was one pothole. Come on, get back on," Hayden said. "You know that old saying about having to get back on the bike."

"No," I said.

"Well, there is one." He grinned and patted the handlebars. "Come on, take two. And this time, when you see giant dips in the road? *Tell* me."

Chapter Four

*M*iss Crossley met me outside the door to her office. "Iced tea?" she offered as we walked inside, where she handed me a tall, icy glass, complete with lemon wedge.

Somehow that made me even more uneasy and suspicious, even though she was having a glass as well, because she was being so nice to me. *Too* nice. "Sure," I said. "Thanks."

"Elizabeth, here's the situation," she began abruptly.

I sipped my iced tea and tried to slow down my breathing. Riding that bike with Hayden had gotten my heart rate up to a slightly dangerous level. Then again, the fact my heart was pounding probably wasn't the bike. It was the fact I had only been here two days and was already getting my second "talking to." It was like being sent to the principal's office, not that I would know much about that, except for a few dress-code violations.

Or maybe it was my encounter with Hayden that was making me feel out of breath. I couldn't explain what it was about him, but we clicked, as if I knew him already, only I didn't. Unless I was his cat, from a former life, reincarnated or something.

"Mr. Talbot Junior and I were talking at lunch," Miss Crossley went on. "We were evaluating our staffing levels, and we seem to have overlooked a few things."

Don't say my qualifications, I thought, *or lack thereof*. "You know, I'm really good at sports," I said. "Is there anything you need help with in that area? I could teach volleyball, or —"

But she wasn't even listening to me, not really. "We realized we have enough housekeepers, if we juggle things a bit. And we don't need you at the front desk, as we thought we did," Miss Crossley said.

"Right," I said slowly.

"And we're covered in the restaurant, we

have enough servers around the clock," she said.

Last hired . . . first fired. I'd heard that phrase before. Was I about to find out what it meant?

They didn't have room for me. They didn't have a job. And all because I was lousy at cleaning my room at home for my entire life. Why hadn't I paid attention when Mom yelled at me all those times?

"Is this just because I didn't get all the sand out of the carpet?" I asked. "Or is it because I sucked that guest's belt into the vacuum? Which completely and kind of ironically damaged the vacuum belt?"

"You did what?"

Oh. So she hadn't even heard about that. I coughed. "We got it out. No problem."

"As I was saying. Every once in a while we discover we're short somewhere," Miss Crossley went on. "So I've rethought your position here. You seem like the perfect person to give this new theory a try."

What new theory? "I do?"

"You have a lot of energy, and you're highly adaptable."

"I am?" This was kind of news to me. Hadn't

· 78 ·

my ex-boyfriend called me the most rigid, uncompromising, stubborn person he ever met?

But that was in a moment of anger, when I broke up with him because I wasn't ready to move things to the next level, and he was, and he wouldn't stop bugging me about it. Which is when my friends and I came up with our theory: You don't really *need* guys. Until you sort of just, you know, want one around. But if he's not good to you and won't listen to you? Forget him. You can do better.

"That's what your recommendations said, that you were a person who could handle anything. Therefore, as of right now, you're the official Tides Inn gofer!" Miss Crossley raised her glass of iced tea in the air, as if to clink against mine in a toast.

"Gopher? Is that like some kind of animal terminology?" I asked. "'Cause I prefer fox, if that's the situation."

Miss Crossley didn't look amused. She never did, around me. "No. It's a—a term. Gofer. Means you will *go for* whatever we need you to," she said.

"You say jump. I say off what?"

She laughed. *Finally*, I thought. I'd made her laugh. She didn't completely hate me, then. "Not exactly, but close. We'll assign you each day based on where we need help. We'll do it on a trial basis. If it doesn't work out . . ."

I thought of the beach, the Inn . . . all the friends and people at home I'd bragged to about this job. No way was I going home. "Oh, it'll work out. I'll be the best gofer ever. In fact, what can I do right now?"

"Well, we're a little shorthanded in the laundry room—got a little bogged down by beach towels," Miss Crossley said. "So if you could help out there, and then run them out to the beach cabana, and see what else needs picking up. And then—well, I'll have to see."

Did I mention I'm about as good at doing laundry as I am at cleaning mirrors? I almost said so, but stopped myself. "Laundry. No problem!" I said cheerfully.

But I couldn't help wondering: Was this job going to be the best thing that could have happened to me, or the worst? Being at Miss Crossley's beck and call could be a little stressful, but I'd rejoice at anything that got me out of vacuuming and cleaning bathrooms, so I wasn't about to complain.

"I think this will work best if we set you up with an exclusive Inn pager," she said. "Only the two of us will have the number. We should have it set up by tomorrow."

"Sounds perfect," I said. But all I could think was that moving from job to job was either going to be very cool, or very Cinderella-like—or some of both.

"What are you doing here, newbie?" Hayden asked when I walked onto the beach later that afternoon. He was standing at the ocean's edge, binoculars around his neck.

"Hi, old person," I said.

"Old person?" he repeated.

"Or is it oldie? If I'm going to be called new all the time, then you can be called old. Right? It only makes sense." I picked up a pink-streaked shell that caught my eye.

"Yeah. Okay. Anyway, what are you doing? Shouldn't you be keeping house, or whatever?"

"Didn't your pal Miss Crossley tell you?

I'm the new go-to girl," I said.

He just stared at me. Actually he was looking me up and down a little, checking me out in my bikini, which I took as a positive thing. He didn't feel the need to look *away*, anyway.

"Hey." I snapped my fingers to get his attention back to my face. "Someone sends me to work on the beach, I dress for the beach. You know?"

I don't mean to sound vain, but I'm not sure his attention was totally on the water, or the people swimming in it. Fortunately for them, another lifeguard was stationed nearby, so there was backup if needed.

I gazed at the water for a moment and spotted a lone figure taking slow, deliberate strokes through the ocean. "Who's that swimming way out there?" I asked.

"Yeah, that's Mr. Anderson. He lives a ways down the beach and he swims a couple of miles every day," Hayden said. "Which would be impressive enough, but then he's at least eighty."

"Wow," I said.

"You're working here now?" Hayden asked. "On the beach?"

"I'm the Tides gofer," I explained. "I go wherever I'm needed." I saluted. "Sounds kind of militaristic, but that's Miss Crossley for you. *Does* she have a background in the military?"

Hayden still looked a little dazed.

"Excuse me. That's 'Peach' to you." I went over to unlock the heavy wooden locker in the dunes and started pulling out beach toys. Chelsea was collecting the kids in the Inn lobby and bringing them down—we were the two "Beach Time Players" for the afternoon, while parents played tennis, went golfing, or just lounged in solitude for a while.

When I turned around to bring a collection of plastic shovels and buckets down to the hard sand, I noticed Hayden was checking out something with his binoculars. *Me*.

I smiled and waved at him, and he quickly pulled them away from his face and turned to face the ocean again. I wasn't sure I wanted him to check me out while I was leaning into a footlocker, but oh well.

"So, uh, when did this new job start?" Hayden asked when I got back to him, pretending he hadn't just been examining me from afar.

"About two hours ago," I said. "Remember that meeting we hurried back for?"

He nodded. "My quads remember." He rubbed his legs as if they were hurting.

"Shut up," I said, pushing him.

"Uh oh. Here come the tykes. You'd better run. Ooh, look, there's Will the Third. Lucky you." He playfully popped me on the arm before heading back up the steps to his lifeguard post.

Okay, so maybe there were going to be challenges to this new position. But if it meant I could hang out by the water—with Hayden nearby? I was all for it.

Chapter Five

"So how's the new job?" Josh asked me when Claire and I ran into him on our way over to the Inn for breakfast the next morning.

"It's okay," I said. "The best part is that I think I'll get to spend more time outdoors."

"Yeah. I wouldn't know about that," Josh said. He was working both as a server in the Inn restaurant and delivering room-service orders. "Although I did get an order yesterday from someone at the beach cabana, so I had to trek down there with a cooler full of beer and soda. It was very tempting to take it down to the beach and shake out a towel and just stay there."

"Except for the losing-your-job part," Claire said.

"Yeah, I started thinking about how much

my textbooks are going to cost. And the guest gave me a huge tip when I got there, so it was worth it."

"It's so gorgeous here. I couldn't leave." I spread out my arms. "The view. The ocean. The salt air."

"You're obsessed with salt air," Claire said.

"I know. I tried to bottle it once, to bring home after our vacation, when I was a kid. Didn't work. So instead I keep buying candles that call themselves ocean breeze and they're so not," I said with a laugh.

"You know what you need to do? That semester-at-sea thing. That's made for you," Claire teased.

I laughed. "I totally should do that. I hear it's really expensive, though."

"Maybe you can get a work-study job. You know, on the ship," Claire said.

"Housekeeping," we said in unison, laughing.

"So what's today's gofer assignment?" Josh asked me.

"I have no idea. I have to wait until I get paged, or Miss Crossley finds me in person."

"That sounds like a real drag," he commented.

"Not always," I said, thinking of the afternoon I'd spent on the beach. Some assignments, like washing towels, were going to be chores. Others were not half bad, especially when they involved hanging out near Hayden. I wasn't completely sure how I felt about him, or whether I should even think about things like that, considering Mark and I weren't "officially" over for good, and considering I didn't even really know Hayden all that well yet.

But I did know that I liked spending time with him, and that I didn't mind looking at him.

Is that shallow of me? Well, okay then, I guess there's a shallow part of me. But honestly, it's 25 percent, at most.

No, really. It's the very top layer.

"Down to the Hull," Josh said as we walked in the side entrance of the Inn. We ate in the basement—literally—the employee kitchen and dining area, which was called the Hull. There was a lot of cute ship imagery around the Inn— well, at least some people thought it was cute.

"Otherwise known as servants' quarters,"

Claire said. "This is how it is in all the old English novels. The maids. In the scullery."

"Scullery? Isn't that on a ship?" I asked.

"And since when am I a maid?" Josh asked. "I'm like way too masculine for that."

"Uh huh." Claire laughed. "I think the scullery is where they hid the people who did all the actual work," she said.

"Let's call this the Hullery then," I said as we walked into the kitchen.

It seemed as if we were the last people to arrive, which made sense considering breakfast was available from seven to eight, and it was nearly eight. Several other people were already sitting around the big, long tables.

"You know who checked in last night?" Caroline was announcing to the room.

"No, who?"

"C. Q. Wallace." She looked smug.

"And that is . . . ," Josh prompted as we picked up bowls, plates, and silverware.

"The famous author, of course," Caroline said. "His last book was in Oprah's book club and number one on Amazon for like a year."

"Still drawing a blank," Josh said.

Caroline let out a loud, exasperated sigh. "You must live under a rock then."

"You know what? I *do*," Josh said. "I'm not used to all this light, actually. My eyes, my eyes!" He shielded his face from the overhead fluorescents.

"Give me a break." Caroline groaned, as we all laughed.

I caught Hayden's eye across the room and smiled, then started to pour myself a bowl of cereal. The cooks sometimes made up chafing dishes of eggs and other hot breakfast treats, like pancakes or potatoes or French toast, for us, but our standard fare was cereal, toast, and fresh fruit. A continental breakfast, according to Miss Crossley.

"What's continental about this? That's one thing I've never understood," I said to Claire as I poured milk over my Frosted Flakes. "Does that mean European? Because I don't think Frosted Flakes are European."

"They must mean this continent then." Claire dropped a few slices of wheat bread into the toaster, while Josh grabbed an orange and a couple of bananas. I followed them to the end of a table to sit down, which just happened to be where Hayden was sitting.

"So how's it going?" Hayden asked.

"Fine. Except of course for the endless initiation tasks," I said.

The night before, we'd been conned into going out to the store for soda and snacks for the entire dorm, after we'd been told it was part of the deal of being newbies.

"Are there any more we should know about, so we can be prepared this time?" Claire asked.

"There's not really any *formal* initiation. You realize that, right?" Caroline asked. "Those guys were just making fun of you."

Was it me, or could she suddenly take the fun out of anything? When had she turned into such a killjoy? I was surprised Zoe wanted to be her roommate. Zoe seemed like she knew how to have fun. Maybe it was the fact I'd seen her boyfriend come to pick her up at the dorm on a motorcycle the night before. That tended to make a person seem daring and adventurous, even when she wore a helmet.

Caroline, on the other end of the spectrum, probably wouldn't even go near a moped or a scooter. It was strange, because she used to be the one who took risks before I did. How did we both change so much?

"Caroline's right. There's no formal anything around here," Hayden said. "But there are traditions, right?"

"Well, I didn't get tossed into the ocean last year when *I* was new," Caroline said primly.

"Oh. Then we'll have to make up for that. You free around nine tonight?" Hayden asked.

"Don't even think about it," Caroline said.

"Okay, but you realize your Tides Inn resume is going to be incomplete," Richard said.

"Like Harvard will care," she said.

"Ooh. Harvard. Impressed," I said sincerely.

She shrugged as if it was no big deal, but at the same time looked pretty pleased with herself. "My parents went there," she said.

"That's right! I remember," I said.

"What—you guys knew each other before now?" Hayden asked.

"Yeah. We both used to come here on vacation when we were ten, eleven," I said. I'd been here five summers in a row, from when I was ten to fifteen, and Caroline had been here three of those summers. "We had cottage rentals next door to each other," I explained. Which might have been the only reason we started hanging out, come to think of it. Proximity. Throughout history, the great friendship maker.

"We actually hung out all the time," I said, just to let Caroline know I hadn't forgotten, even if she had. I don't know why it mattered so much to me. I guess it's that I can't stand being snobbed by someone I already know. Like when you talk to a guy from school at a party, at length, about all kinds of personal stuff, and then you see him the next day and he's with his friends and acts like it never happened. Like he barely even knows your name. I hate that. When I'd first seen Caroline, in my first panicky moments, I'd had this hope that she might make it easier for me to blend in. Quite the opposite had happened. I was blending in just fine, but it was no thanks to her.

"So you guys go way back. That's very interesting," Hayden said.

"Well, we're not the only people here who

know each other from before," Caroline said. "Zoe and Hayden are from the same town, and—"

"Not exactly the same town," Hayden explained. "Neighboring. We went to the same high school, that's all."

"Private day school," Caroline corrected him.

"Huh," I said. "Is that the famous Maple Leaf Academy?" I teased.

"Mapleville," Hayden said.

"Ah. Of course. Very interesting."

"Is it?" Hayden asked.

"Sure." I finished my bowl of cereal and walked over to set it in the sink.

"Did you know?" Hayden asked as he came up behind me.

"About you and Zoe?" I said.

He looked a little confused. "About me and Zoe what?"

"Going to the same private school," I said. "No, I didn't—"

"That's not what I meant." He set a plate and knife into the sink next to my bowl. "I was going to tell you that new people around here do all the dishes. Did anyone tell you yet?"

"Yeah, right," I scoffed.

"No, seriously," he insisted. "You fill up the dish racks over there, then carry them upstairs to the main kitchen—"

"Okay, so when do we get to be *not* the new people anymore?" I asked him. "Is there like a day of amnesty?"

"Yeah, this isn't a fraternity, you know," Claire added. "You can't keep hazing us forever."

"We're not doing anything that bad! Just teasing. Come on, lighten up," Hayden said to me.

"Yeah, well, it's not actually all that funny," I said, trying to keep a straight face. Because I wasn't mad, and I didn't care. They could ask us to do the dishes all they wanted, but it didn't mean we would.

"It's not funny?" Hayden asked, wrinkling his nose.

"No."

"Really."

"Really," I said. "It's getting old. Tired. Kind of sad."

We just looked at each other for a few seconds. His eyes were this deep, dark-blue steel gray, the kind that seem impossible to read.

"Liza. Liza? Liza!"

I think it took three tries before I actually heard my name being called, though it could have been more, because I wasn't paying attention to anything but Hayden for a minute.

Oh no, I thought as I turned around and saw Miss Crossley standing in the doorway. There were a couple of problems here. One, I was feeling this incredible pull toward Hayden, suspiciously like an undertow. I'd have to move from the spot where I was standing or I could be in trouble.

Problem Two, Miss Crossley was here looking for me. That might not be good.

"I was hoping I'd find you," she said. She snapped her fingers in front of my eyes. "But I'm a little concerned. Are you awake yet?"

"Sure—of course," I said.

"Well, you seem a little out of it."

"Just about to have my first cup of coffee. I'll be lively in no time," I promised. "Hyper, even." I shuffled over to the giant coffee urn and poured myself a cup to go. I had a feeling my breakfast was about to be over.

Miss Crossley nodded. "That's more like it. You're not staying up late, getting into trouble, are you?"

Not yet, I thought. "Of course not," I assured her.

"Well. Good morning, everyone." Miss Crossley surveyed the Hullery, nodding to different people.

"Hey, Peach," Hayden said.

"Hayden. You know how I feel about that," Miss Crossley said.

"Sorry, Miss Crossley. I'll knock it off, as requested." Hayden came over beside me and refilled his coffee cup.

"Now, Liza, I've reviewed our staffing for the day and I've figured out exactly where we need you," Miss Crossley said.

Why did I get a feeling of intense dread when she said that? *Please don't say housekeeping. Or laundry. Or something even yuckier.* It didn't help that across the kitchen, Caroline was sitting there with a smug smile on her face, like she couldn't wait to hear where I'd be stuck.

"I hope you packed an ample supply of sunscreen." Miss Crossley smiled at me. "We need you to pull some more beach duty. The tots group will be on the beach this morning, so we need extra hands for supervision. Be dressed and on the beach by nine."

"Okay, sounds great. Thanks!" I said, smiling at her—and at Caroline. If she thought I was suffering under this new arrangement, she was wrong.

"Now," Miss Crossley said. "Caroline, could you follow me back upstairs? I need to go over a few things with you regarding a very special guest."

"Oh, of *course*." Caroline pushed back her chair.

I happily sipped my coffee. Now I had even more of a reason to be glad Caroline had the front-desk job instead of me. I got to be outside all day, while she had to be watched by Miss Crossley, and deal with "very special"— translation, very demanding—guests.

"The beach, huh? Interesting," Hayden commented. He sipped from his coffee cup. "You're new here, so do you know how to get to the beach?"

I could have swatted him, except that he was smiling at me in that impossible-to-resist way. "I'm pretty sure I know. You just follow the boardwalk, right?" I asked, returning his smile.

"Come on, Liza—let's go," Claire said, tugging at my arm. "I forgot my key and I need to get changed for sailing."

"Here." I started to hand my key to her, but she pushed my hand away.

"You have to get changed anyway," she said.

"Oh. Right. Okay. Well, see you in a while," I said to Hayden.

Claire and I walked up the steps and out the side entrance. "I didn't really forget my key," Claire confessed on our way back to the dorm. "But I had to ask—what's going on with you guys?"

"Who?"

"*Who?* Are you serious?" Claire cried. "You and Hayden, who else? You were oblivious to the world for a few seconds there, when Miss Crossley came in."

"Oh, that? It's nothing. I was just sleepy."

"I don't think it's nothing," Claire said. "I think it's something."

I laughed. "Have you ever seen that segment on David Letterman? 'Is this something, or is this nothing?'"

Claire didn't laugh. She looked so serious, though, that it almost made me crack up again. "Remember what my sister said. Beware of hookups. It could ruin your whole summer. And Hayden doesn't strike me as the kind of guy to just have *one* hookup per summer. That's all I'm saying."

"Don't worry. I'm not planning on getting involved with Hayden," I said.

Then again, who said you had to plan everything in life?

And how well did she know Hayden? Just because he was good-looking and sort of a flirt, that didn't mean he'd play the field. The beach, maybe. But not the field.

"I'm sorry," Claire said as we walked into our room. "I don't mean to tell you what to do."

"No, it's okay—we're friends. I don't mind the advice."

"You sure?"

"Yeah."

"Good. I know I'm ultraconservative about everything. You must think I'm totally boring," Claire said.

"Not at all!" I said. "We're just kind of different, that's all. But it's a good different. You're looking out for me, and I appreciate that." Then I set to deciding which swimsuit I wanted to wear.

When I got to the beach, I found out Chelsea and I would be working together again. We were supposed to have a large group of children, but apparently a few parents had changed their minds and canceled, because we only had three kids to look after. Which was a pretty sweet ratio, if you were a kid—and made it easy for us. They were brothers, ages five, seven, and eight, and assured us they were excellent swimmers.

"We believe you, we do," I said. "But we're

going to hang around and swim with you, because we get hot, too, okay?"

"All right," the oldest one groaned.

I pulled off my sweatshirt and helped Chelsea haul out the toys. We set up the kids with an assortment of shovels, buckets, levelers—everything they needed to make the biggest sand castle ever, which they'd told me was their plan.

Chelsea ran back up to the Inn to get some breakfast because she'd overslept. I was standing on the wet sand beside the kids, keeping an eye out but not interfering, when I saw Hayden, out of the corner of my eye, climbing down from his lifeguard stand. This should be good, I thought.

"So. You found the beach," he said as he walked toward me.

"Found it just as I left it. Really sandy," I said.

He looked me up and down, appraising my second swimsuit of the summer. (I'd brought four, which sounds excessive, but isn't, especially when you buy them on sale.) This one was a smallish bikini, with a bright striped pattern.

"Did you bring enough sunscreen? I have some you could borrow," he offered.

"Shouldn't you be keeping your eye on the water?" I commented. "People might be drowning."

"I'm on a break," Hayden said.

"I guess they could be newbies, so let 'em drown, right?" I teased.

"Hey, I never said that. *Hey.*"

"No, but you implied it. But if someone drowns, no problem. The new people will perform CPR," I said.

"You know CPR?" he asked, looking impressed.

"And if there are jellyfish? The newbies will go swimming and get stung," I went on.

"Well, probably, because you won't notice you're swimming with them until it's too late," Hayden said.

"So we're not just new, we're clueless now." I nodded. "Nice."

"Hey, I don't think that." He took my arm

and started to pull me toward the water. "Of course as an *old* person, I'd know better than to stand so close to the water when it's still only sixty degrees, but . . ."

"Don't throw me in. *Don't!*" I cried, struggling to hold my ground. I dug my heels into the sand.

"Why not?" he said. "Give me one good reason—"

"Because I'll throw *you* in," I said. "And how would it look for the lifeguard to—hey!"

He'd grabbed my ankle and was about to lift me over his head.

"Quit it!" I said, dancing away from him.

You know how some people have chemistry? That was us. In like triplicate. To the nth degree.

I checked on the kids to make sure they were still okay—which they were. While I was talking to them, Hayden picked me up from behind.

"No fair!" I cried, pounding on his back with my fists as he spun around, twirling me with him. "Do not throw me in. Do you hear me? I'll come after you at night when you least expect it and—"

Over Hayden's shoulder I noticed Caroline had come to the end of the boardwalk, but she hadn't progressed any farther. Her sunglasses were lowered on the bridge of her nose as if she needed to get a better look at something. Or someone. Us?

What was she doing away from the reception desk, anyway? She never strayed from there—she considered herself too important to be replaced.

"And what?" Hayden asked. "Keep going."

"I think someone wants to borrow your binoculars," I said to Hayden. "Put me down, okay? This time I really mean it."

"What?" Hayden asked.

I went to point out where Caroline was standing, but she wasn't there anymore.

"Likely story. Caroline was out here?" Hayden scoffed. "I'm sure."

"She *was*," I insisted. "And here's proof." I pointed to the boardwalk, where Miss Crossley was now making an appearance. It was like a runway in a bad fashion show.

Except Miss Crossley wasn't turning back. She marched across the sand toward me, still in her shoes, a pair of shiny brown penny loafers, which she wore with plaid Bermuda shorts and a white oxford cloth shirt.

"Liza, are you paying attention to the children?" she asked.

"Of course I am," I said. I turned around to get Hayden to vouch for me, but he was already gone, disappeared up the steps to his lifeguard post. So much for backup.

"Where is Chelsea?" Miss Crossley demanded.

"She'll be right back. Honestly, Miss Crossley. I was watching three kids build a sand castle, at low tide. I've never let them out of my sight. Right, guys?"

The kids were too busy digging to respond.

I looked back at Miss Crossley and shrugged. "You know kids, they never—"

"Is that a pierced belly button?" she asked.

Wasn't it obvious? I could lie, and say I'd fallen on a staple or something, but what would be the point? "Yes?" I said tentatively.

"Hm. That's against dress code policy, Liza.

No untraditional piercings."

I shook my head. "I'm sorry, Miss Crossley, but I never *got* all the stuff about dress code policy. I didn't know."

"Now you do. I'll be happy to give you any handouts you're missing. But Liza. Doesn't common *sense* tell you not to pierce your belly button?"

"I guess not," I said. "At least, not . . . *my* common sense," I murmured.

"You'll either need to cover it up or remove it," she said.

"I'll take it out," I promised.

"Good. And Liza? I'm watching you." She made this weird hand motion from her eyes to me, and back again, repeating it a few times. Not only was she sort of a taskmaster, she was nerdy, too.

No, Caroline's watching me, I thought as I crouched down to help the kids build their castle. *And I don't know why, but I'll find out.*

Chapter Six

"Kind of slow at the front desk this morning?" I asked Caroline once I made it up to the Inn on my lunch break. Brittany had come down to the beach to relieve first Chelsea, then me.

Caroline looked up from the women's magazine she'd been reading at her desk. "What's that?" She was wearing the Inn uniform all of us had—polo shirt, khaki shorts—but she had a fancy silk scarf tied around her neck, to dress it up, I guess.

"Oh, I just thought I saw you on the beach a while ago," I said. "Which was sort of odd, considering that your job is in here."

She flipped a page of the magazine with her nicely manicured nails. "I was checking the tide. People kept asking me what the surf was like, if there were any good waves."

"Huh. Really," I commented.

"Yes," she said. "The phone was ringing off the hook with people asking."

"Really," I said again.

"You know, you should be wearing shorts and a T-shirt," she said. "Inn policy. No one's allowed in the lobby looking like that, least of all staff."

"It's a bikini top and a skirt. I'll get dressed in a sec," I promised, adjusting the big white beach towel tied around my waist, which at least covered my frowned-upon belly button ring. "This is an Inn towel, so doesn't that count for something?"

"You're in a bikini, so no, and it's not a skirt," she said. "In fact, if you wouldn't mind stepping away from the desk? I don't want a guest walking in to be offended."

I stared at her. "There's something offensive about me now?"

"No! Of course not. I just meant—you know, not everyone's comfortable around people who aren't dressed. That's all," she said.

"Uh huh." I wasn't buying it. I believe in being the tiniest bit blunt, when someone won't 'fess up. "Caroline, what gives?" I asked her.

"What are you talking about?"

"What do you have against me?" I asked.

"What? Nothing." She kept flipping through her magazine, not making eye contact with me.

"I mean, I haven't seen you in a long time. Did I do something to offend you, the last time we hung out? I hope you're not holding a grudge over something I did way back when," I said.

"Of course I'm not," she said. "I wouldn't be that petty."

I raised my eyebrows. *Really,* I thought. *Are you sure?*

She laughed. "Look, is this because I took the front-desk job away from you?"

"That's a whole separate issue, actually," I said. "But no. I'm glad I have my job, even if I don't know what it's going to be from day to day."

"I'd hate that," Caroline said.

Of course you would, I thought. *You're too*

inflexible to move around from place to place.

Caroline also struck me as the kind of person who couldn't stand to get her hands dirty. She'd never want to build sand castles and jump over waves with the little kids. And she'd for sure never want to have to clean someone else's room.

Not that I wanted to do that, either.

"So why were you out on the beach a while ago as if you were spying on me? And why did Miss Crossley—who, from what I can tell, practically never leaves the building—come running out as soon as you went back inside?" I asked. "What did you tell her?"

"Nothing. She was on her way out when I was on my way in," Caroline said.

I thought about that for a second. It could be true, I supposed, but it was quite a coincidence. I decided I'd wasted enough of my lunch hour on this, and I was about to step away from the desk when she said, "Liza? It's just— you should know. Hayden and Zoe? They dated last summer. Like, very seriously."

"Oh." This was kind of big news to me, but

kind of not. I'd seen the way Hayden and Zoe acted around each other, sort of awkward and maybe a little annoyed. Which I could see was the way exes acted, now that I knew about it. I briefly wondered who broke up with whom, and when. No doubt Caroline was dying to tell me, but I wouldn't give her the satisfaction of asking. Anyway, I could get the information straight from Hayden, if I really wanted to know. And I wasn't sure I did.

Caroline was watching me for some sort of stunned, or pained, reaction.

Instead I just shrugged. "Well, okay. What about that? I mean, why tell me?"

"I just thought you'd want to know. They were really close."

"Okay," I said.

"Really close," she repeated.

I figured she was trying to say, in her Caroline way, that they'd slept together. "I don't see how it really matters, but okay, now I know." I shrugged. "What other news you got?"

"What do you mean?" Caroline asked.

I leaned forward on the desk. "Tell me

about Miss Crossley. Who did she date last summer?"

Caroline glared at me. "Ha ha. You think you're so funny."

"Come on, if you're spilling gossip, tell me everything. In fact, who did *you* date last summer? If I don't have the background on every single person here, I won't feel comfortable," I said. "I mean, this is the kind of stuff I was looking for that night at the bonfire. The dirt on everyone. But no one said anything."

The phone rang and Caroline grabbed it on the first ring, no doubt to avoid my question. "Thank you for calling the Tides Inn, my name is Caroline, how may I assist you?" she said in a sugary-sweet tone.

She had the perfect phony voice to be answering the phone. I would never have been able to match that, so she probably did deserve the front-desk job over me.

What was Caroline so worried about? Zoe was seeing Brandon-with-a-motorcycle now, so it wasn't as if Caroline had to look out for her best friend's interests.

Does *Caroline* have a crush on Hayden? I

wondered. Is that why she's being so rude to me, and why she wants me to stay away from him? Is that why she's spying on us?

If that were true, maybe she felt like she deserved him, since she'd known him longer.

Still, I couldn't picture her and Hayden together. He seemed too loud and adventurous and fun, and she seemed too rigid and, well, unfun.

But if she truly liked him, I could let her have him. I could wait until she got off the phone, and tell her not to worry, that Hayden was all hers and I'd keep my distance.

Except I didn't want to do that. So I walked out of the lobby onto the back porch, stretched my arms over my head, and took a deep, satisfying breath of the fresh salty air. I couldn't wait to get back onto the beach.

"Do you have to look so happy?"

I turned and saw a man sitting in one of the wicker chairs, near the edge of the porch. He had his feet up on the railing and a computer on his lap. He looked like he was in his forties, with slightly graying black hair, longish sideburns, and wore a loose linen shirt and jeans.

"I'm sorry?" I asked.

"You look too unbearably happy. And must you breathe so loudly? You even *breathe* happily," he commented.

"I just really enjoy the way the air smells here." Or, at least I *did*, I thought as I fanned the cigarette smoke away from my face. "What are those, clove cigarettes?" I asked.

"No, they're Turkish."

"Mm." Cool-sounding, but still cancer-causing, I was guessing.

I remembered Miss Crossley's instructions on our first day. *You don't have to smoke with the guests, but you do have to offer them a light.* Fortunately, this guy didn't need one.

"It's impossible to concentrate around here, with so much coming and going," he said. "And nobody told me this place would be full of children."

I was going to point out that he shouldn't sit on the entrance facing the beach, where everyone had to walk past, if he wanted privacy. But that seemed obvious—not to mention a little obnoxious. "I don't know, it's still kind of early in the season. I don't think there are *that* many kids. What are you trying to concentrate on?" I asked.

"Writing," he said.

"Oh. Oh!" I hadn't recognized him at first, but of course—it was the writer Caroline had mentioned at breakfast.

"And it's only June, and this is the sixth place I've stayed already this summer, and I haven't been able to write a word at any of them. Though that's not your fault. I mean, it is, but it isn't."

I laughed. "How is it my fault—like, at all?"

"It isn't. I was just grasping at straws. Speaking of straws, here we are now." He nodded at Daunte, who was carrying a tray toward us.

Daunte smiled at me on his way past, then set a tall glass on the table and had the guest sign the bill before heading back inside.

He grimaced as he drank it. "Horrible, awful stuff."

"What is it exactly?" I asked.

"Quintuple espresso, on ice, with a splash of grenadine and a lemon wedge."

The description alone was enough to turn my stomach. "And it's bad?" I asked. "Should I get you another one? Here—let me do that. I'll run to the kitchen," I offered.

"No, it's not the way it's made. I mean, it's supposed to taste ghastly. And it does, so I can't complain to the bartender."

"Barista," I said.

"Whatever," he said. "As long as it works, I don't care." He took another gulp and made a face. "Something has to work. Or else I'll have to pack, again, and move to yet another hotel for inspiration."

"How would moving help? I mean, how do you know this *isn't* the right place to write your next book? It could be the perfect spot, if you just give it a chance."

"Your optimism is tedious. But I'll take it." He looked over at me. "What's your name?"

"Liza."

He reached over to shake my hand. "C. Q. Wallace."

I wanted to ask what the C. Q. stood for, but I decided that would be rude. If a person chose to go by his initials, there must be a reason—probably that he didn't like his name. Anyway, I could get the information out of Caroline later. If she was still speaking to me.

"You work here?" he asked.

"No, I just offered to run to the kitchen for you because I'm such an optimist," I said.

He laughed and lifted his coffee cup. "Touché."

Chapter Seven

*T*hat night I ran up to the shuttle van just as Hayden was pulling away from the Inn. The van was always parked right out front, on the circular drive, and I'd caught him just before he left. I was panting and out of breath as I knocked on the window to get his attention.

Hayden lowered the window and stared at me. "What are you doing here?"

I waved my pager in the air, because I was temporarily unable to speak.

He leaned out the window. "You need a new pager?" he asked.

I shook my head. "Town. Have to . . . go to . . . town."

"Okay . . . Well, don't die on me. Get in."

I walked around and climbed up into the front seat of the van. Then I slicked my wet hair back from my face.

"Were you summoned out of the ocean?" Hayden asked.

I laughed. "Almost. I had just gotten out of the shower when Miss Crossley paged me."

"And what did she want? Did she say I needed company? An assistant, maybe, to carry all the luggage? 'Cause that would be nice."

"No!" I laughed. "I called and she said to come to her office, so I did and then she hands me this pen. And tells me I have to go to town with you and find more pens like this. And she tells me I have like thirty seconds before you leave for the train station. I tried to tell her I had a car here and I could drive, but she said this was official Inn business, so I should take the official Inn van—"

"No problem. There's a small office supply store near the train station," Hayden said.

"Oh. Okay," I panted. "Then it doesn't completely not make sense. You could have gone there, though, couldn't you? I mean, why didn't she ask you to just run in and get the pens?" I asked.

"I see. Trying to get out of work already." Hayden nodded. "You've only been a gofer for a couple days and you're already trying *not* to go for stuff?"

"No!" I said. Then I laughed. I seemed to do that a lot around him. Was he that funny, or was I that nervous? "Well, maybe."

"No, I know what it is. Miss C. probably didn't want me to leave the van, in case the train comes and nobody's there to meet the guests. Although that's completely ridiculous, because the train is almost never early. In fact, it's usually late by a few minutes." He pulled out onto the main road into town. I was busy combing my hair and squeezing the ends to wring out some of the extra water.

"Do you need a towel?" Hayden asked.

"No, that's okay. I can just dry my hair this way." I opened the window and let the warm evening air rush over me. The day had been one of the warmest yet, which was why I'd needed an extra swim, which was why I'd needed an extra shower. I'd even postponed dinner, preferring instead to spend the time in the water bodysurfing. Of course, now it was looking like I wouldn't eat at all, given that it was about a half hour trip to the train station, and by the time we got back it would be close to nine. But I could always sneak into the Hull and grab a bowl of cereal, at least.

"So. Pens," Hayden said. "Miss Crossley had a sudden urgent need for pens."

I shrugged. "I guess."

"Uh huh. She doesn't strike me as the kind of person who ever runs out of things," Hayden commented. "You know what I mean?"

What was he getting at? "What, you think I made this up? I didn't!" I said. "If I wanted to go with you, I would have just asked."

"Really."

"Really," I said. "Anyway, like I said, I have a car here. Last time I tried to start it, though, it wouldn't start. But let's say I did want to go to town. I'd drive that," I said.

"If it started," he said.

"Right." It was difficult to be indignant when you drove an old, slightly dented, slightly-to-very-unreliable car. And your hair was wet, and your hair made the back of your shirt wet, and you had thrown on jeans that were clinging to you because the night was so hot. And they weren't even your favorite jeans to begin with.

"So how many guests are we picking up?" I asked.

Hayden grabbed a slip of paper on the dashboard of the van. "Lyle, party of four."

"How does this work? Do they pay you? Do they tip you?" I asked.

"Tips are welcome and appreciated," Hayden said in a monotone voice.

I laughed.

"That's what it says in every other shuttle van or bus I've ever been in, but not this one," Hayden said. "But people seem to know, anyway. I carry their luggage, I tell them whatever they want to know about the Inn, the area, my college plans."

"You're like a tour guide," I said.

"Kind of. I guess," he said.

"You're the first impression they get of the Inn." I checked out his official Tides Inn polo shirt, khaki shorts, and Tides Inn ball cap. "You're dressed for the part. Shoot. I probably should be, too."

"No, that's okay. I'll just tell them you're some random girl I picked up on the way," Hayden said.

"Oh, thanks." I laughed. "That's how I dream of being known."

"And you obviously got caught in the rain. Not that there's been any rain," he said.

"Tell them you saw me swimming to town— no, drowning in the ocean—and you pulled over to offer me a ride."

"Good. That's good." He nodded. "Okay, so we've got our story straight."

"I'm surprised Miss C. didn't tell me I should be better dressed. She was a little frantic," I said. "Like, really stressed about these pens."

"Whenever she gets like that, it's usually because of a guest. So maybe those pens aren't for her, maybe they're for someone staying at the Inn," Hayden suggested.

I looked at the pen, twirling it back and forth in my palm. "You know what? You're right. I bet these are for that famous writer, C. Q. Wallace. You know, the guy Caroline mentioned? I actually met him and talked to him this afternoon."

"What's he like?" Hayden asked.

"What's that word that means someone's kind of rude . . . but funny? You know, someone who sits around and complains about everything," I said.

"What was he complaining about?"

"Writer's block."

"Wait a second. Didn't he have some huge best-selling book? Isn't that what Caroline said?"

"I guess. I don't know. Is there a bookstore in town where we could check out his books?"

"There is, but I doubt we'll have time tonight," Hayden said. "What with the emergency pens and all. Maybe another expedition, another night." He glanced over at me as he stopped at a red light.

What was he implying? Was he asking me

out—sort of? I wondered. "Sure," I said slowly.

And then he just sat there and stared at me for a few seconds, without saying anything. As if there was something about my face he was trying to memorize, in case he had to describe me or pick me out of a police lineup. I could feel this heat on my face, and it had nothing to do with the warm evening.

"Um, I think you can go now," I said, gesturing to the stoplight. "The light's green."

"Yeah, of course." Hayden coughed and turned his attention back to driving.

"Told you the train would be late."

I walked out of the small office supply store to find Hayden standing on the sidewalk, waiting for me, clutching an ice cream cone in each hand.

"Curmudgeon," I said.

"What?" Hayden laughed. "What did you just call me?"

"Not you. The guy who needs these pens." I held up the small brown bag that contained a dozen of the special pens. "I just thought of the word I was trying to think of before to describe him," I explained.

"Curmudgeon. Okay." Hayden held out one of the ice cream cones to me. "You like chocolate? Everyone likes chocolate, right? Which is what I was thinking. See, I was going to get a vanilla and a chocolate, to give you a choice, but then, if you chose chocolate, I'd be stuck with vanilla, which would suck."

"Always thinking of others, aren't you?" I asked.

"Hey, I can eat both of them," Hayden offered.

"What? No way." I took the waffle cone from him. "I'm starving—thanks. How did you know I missed dinner?"

"I didn't," Hayden said. "Anyway, it's not like you can't have dinner and ice cream."

"How much do I owe you?" I asked.

Hayden shook his head. "No problem."

"No, seriously," I said, taking a few dollars out of my pocket.

"Don't even." He pushed my hand away. "Save it for your next trip to the coffee shop."

"Okay. It's a deal. I'll treat next time we

both happen to be there at the same time," I offered.

"We could always go together. To make things easier," Hayden pointed out.

He was doing that thing again, where it seemed like he might be asking me out, but I wasn't sure.

"Hm. Yeah, I guess we could. If we ever get the same break schedule again." That was seeming a little doubtful, since I wasn't going to know my breaks ahead of time. Of course, I could ask Hayden for his cell number, so I could call him whenever I did have time to meet at the coffee shop, but that seemed a little aggressive.

But I did have some questions I wanted to ask him. Since we were hanging out on a bench at the train station, eating our ice cream, now seemed as good a time as any.

"So, you and Zoe," I said. "You guys went out?"

"How'd you find out about that?" he asked.

"Caroline."

"Ah. And she told you because . . ."

I shrugged. "I have no idea. I didn't ask, if

that's what you're implying."

"I wasn't."

"Okay, good. Well, she's quite the gossip, then."

"Yeah, and that's exactly why I was pissed when she got that front-desk job instead of you."

"You were?"

"She'll try to keep tabs on everyone, and she'll turn everything into a story that she just can't wait to tell everyone else. She's one of those . . . I don't know. My mom would call her a busybody."

"So. There's no story?" I asked.

"Sure, there's a story, but it's pretty short. We dated," Hayden said. "It was weird, because back home, we go to the same school—"

"The vaunted Maple Syrup Academy," I interjected.

"Maple*ville*. And we never even talked much there. Anyway, we went out for a while here, then it started to kind of be not that much fun anymore."

"Don't you hate it when that happens?"

"It happened to you?" Hayden asked.

"Sure. Once or twice, anyway," I said.

"So, are you—you know—seeing anyone right now? You have a boyfriend stashed at home?"

"Stashed? Like, where. Under the bed?" I joked. Then I realized that was kind of an unfortunate, misleading choice of words. "Not quite." I could tell him about Mark, but I wasn't sure I needed to, at least not yet. Anyway, we were on an official break, so Mark wasn't technically my boyfriend right now. He was my boyfriend-in-limbo.

"How about you?" I asked, turning the question back on Hayden.

"I don't have any boyfriends at home, if that's what you're asking," he said.

"I wasn't." Though I guess I could have, if I didn't know about him and Zoe.

"No girlfriends, either." He tossed the napkin into the trashcan.

Okay, so we'd established that we both were available. Now what? Some people weren't seeing anyone, but that didn't necessarily mean they were available. Hayden could have sworn off dating, or he could be waiting for the perfect girl, or waiting until he got to college to have another girlfriend, or something like that. Because why start something now, when it was bound to implode in September? Then again, why not start something now—knowing it would be short-term?

Wow. There were two ways to approach this thing with Hayden. If it *was* a thing. If it had potential, the way I thought it did. The way he looked at me sometimes, I was pretty sure he felt the same way, that this could turn into something if we decided to go for it.

Lighten up, Liza, I thought to myself as I heard the train approaching from a distance. The guy bought you an ice cream cone. Nobody's saying this is destiny. It's about pens. I sort of wanted to ask him if he wanted to go to the beach later, when we got back to the Inn, but I thought it would be smartest to wait awhile and see where I stood with him before I got in any deeper.

That love undertow could pull you in and drag you out to sea if you weren't careful.

"If you could take the train anywhere, where would you go?" Hayden asked as we both walked up toward the opening doors, looking for the shuttle passengers. Hayden pulled a TIDES INN sign out of his back pocket and held it up, smiling at everyone who was disembarking.

"The train. Does that mean London's out?" I asked.

"Most definitely. Think a little closer to home." Hayden waved to one of the conductors. "Hey, how's it going?"

"Then somewhere west. How about Montana?" I said.

"You guys go to Montana?" Hayden called to the conductor.

Chapter Eight

"*W*ould you like that toasted?"

"Yes, with a smidgen of butter, and do you have any jam?"

"Packets right there, ma'am." I smiled as I dropped an English muffin into the toaster.

Miss Crossley hadn't even bothered to page me. She'd personally walked over to the dorm, pounded on my door to wake me up, then told me to be at the Inn by seven A.M. to work in the restaurant minicafé—more like a kiosk—for breakfast, because Julia had called in sick.

Never mind that I didn't know how to make decent coffee—Zoe was doing that. No, I was in charge of serving up muffins, bagels, and Danishes, and manning the cash register.

Considering how much the guests paid to stay at the Inn, I would have thought all their food was on the house, but apparently not. They were all too willing to fork over five dollars for a muffin and a cup of coffee. Then again, if they had enough money to stay at the Inn? Money probably wasn't an issue for them. And five dollars wasn't going to break them, the way it might break me, in the last few days before our first paychecks.

The little café was located on the left-hand side of the Inn, the opposite end from the restaurant. It was sort of out of the way, but I kept looking around, wondering if I'd catch a glimpse of Claire, who said she'd come visit me—before she rolled over and went back to sleep, that is—or Josh, or maybe Hayden.

Then again, if Hayden knew Zoe worked here, would he come by? Were they at the stage of avoiding each other, or was that long past?

"Do you usually work here?" I asked Zoe between customers. "I thought you worked in the restaurant."

"I do both," she said. "Three days a week I'm

there, three days I'm here. Usually. Sometimes it's more time here and less there, or whatever."

"You don't make as much here, right? No tips," I commented.

"That's true, but you get a higher hourly wage, so it works out," she said.

"Oh, right, of course," I said as if I knew that already. But I hadn't thought about it. That made me wonder: What would my hourly wage be, since I worked at a different job nearly every hour? Did I get paid for doing things like running out on emergency pen errands? Or was that just considered fun?

I didn't need to be paid to hang out with Hayden, I could tell Miss Crossley. But if she wanted to do that, then fine by me. Depending on how I looked at it, either the money, or Hayden, was a bonus.

I thought about the way he'd looked at me a couple of times the night before, like when we were stopped in traffic, and how he was waiting for me outside the store, ice cream cone in hand.

"Excuse me, Miss."

I came back to the present and noticed a man was waving his hand in front of my face.

"Oh. Sorry, sir. What can we get you?" I asked him with a friendly smile.

He ordered a coffee and a bagel, which I got right to toasting.

"Space much?" Zoe asked me as she started preparing his café latte. "Were you out late last night?"

"No," I said, but I felt an embarrassed blush on my cheeks. Being caught daydreaming about someone's ex-boyfriend, while she's standing right there . . . that's a little tacky, no?

"Well, I was," Zoe said under her breath. "Great party, over at a friend of Brandon's beach house."

"No kidding? Hey, how long have you guys been together?" I asked. If I could find that out, maybe I'd learn how long she and Hayden had been apart. I didn't know how that would help me, so maybe I was just being nosy.

"Oh, uh, since the end of last summer, I guess. And then sort of off and on, you know, because he lives here, and I don't. I was gone during the school year."

"Hey, guys." Josh walked up to the kiosk and leaned on the counter. "Some guy just called room service and ordered a quintuple iced espresso. Could you make that for me?" he asked.

"Sure," Zoe said. "No problem."

"I've never even *heard* of that many espresso shots. He wants me to bring fresh lemon wedges, too. And he wants it delivered to his room as soon as possible, as if that's new, I mean, who doesn't want things right away when they call room service. And he was completely grumpy about it, like I should know what he wanted before he even said it, and I should know who he is without him telling me."

I smiled. "I think I know who that is."

"Yeah. Me too. Room three-oh-one." Zoe took the order from Josh and started to make the drink. "He ordered the same thing yesterday."

"C. Q. Wallace," I said. "The writer."

Josh didn't look enthused.

"I hear he tips really well," Zoe added.

"And he's a writer?" Josh asked, sounding skeptical.

"A best-selling one, according to Caroline," I said. "She's supposedly read all his books." I caught myself before I said anything really nasty about Caroline; after all, I was working with her roommate today. "Anyway, he mentioned yesterday that he's having trouble with his newest book. Writer's block or something like that."

"Tell him I hope this works," Zoe said as she placed the iced drink on Josh's tray.

We were busy for the next five minutes, and then Josh reappeared.

"You won't believe this. He asked if I knew who someone named Eliza was," Josh said. "I told him this wasn't *My Fair Lady*, and your name wasn't Eliza, it was Liza, and yeah, I knew you." He took an envelope off his tray and handed it to me.

I unsealed the envelope, which was Tides Inn stationery, and pulled out a folded beige sheet of paper. When I opened it, a twenty-dollar bill fell out.

"You know, I'm the one who made his coffee," Zoe joked.

Thanks for the pens.
Now what am I going to use them for?
Well, there's always the crossword.
Uninspiringly and gratefully yours,
C.Q.W.

"Twenty bucks. Cool." I explained about the errand I'd gone on the evening before.

Zoe had been reading the note over my shoulder. "Just for buying some pens?"

"They weren't just pens. They're very special pens."

"What did you do, drive to Providence for him?" Zoe asked.

"No, I—" But I didn't get a chance to tell her, because suddenly there was a line. It was probably just as well, I decided as I reached into the pastry case. No point telling her about me and Hayden—since there *was* no "me and Hayden." Not yet, anyway.

* * *

"Hayden! You're not going to believe this." I started to climb up the lifeguard tower, but halfway up, I stopped.

Hayden was looking at me as if he didn't recognize me, so I paused for a second. Were his sunglasses too dark or something? Was he watching swimmers?

"Hayden?" I said.

"Yeah," he said in a monotone. He seemed embarrassed to be seen talking to me. He kept looking over my shoulder at something, or someone.

I looked down at my outfit and laughed. "Okay, so probably I could take off the apron now. I had to play coffee-shop girl this morning. Well, not coffee shop exactly, more like coffee kiosk."

"Right." Hayden didn't find me all that amusing, apparently. Was he in a bad mood, or what?

"Hey, is everything okay?" I asked.

"Sure." He shrugged.

"Really?"

"Yeah."

I didn't exactly believe him, but I didn't want to press the issue, either. If he wanted to talk, he would. "Okay, well, you're still not going to believe this. We've been rewarded." I held up the twenty-dollar bill. "And all for a dozen pens. I thought maybe we could split the reward and go for coffee at Sally's later. I owe you."

"What? No, you don't," he said.

"Yes, for the ice cream, remember?"

He might be remembering it, but he wasn't admitting it. "I can't really talk right now. I've got to watch the water."

"Right. Okay, I'll see you later."

That was weird. He hadn't asked where I was working that afternoon or whether I'd be coming to the beach. He hadn't actually seemed to care whether I even existed.

I didn't expect him to do cartwheels over a twenty-dollar tip, but as far as I was concerned, it was pretty cool. I thought we sort of bonded the night before—at least as friends, if nothing else. Now he was acting about as warm as, say, the ocean in February.

I threw my blue apron over my shoulder and headed down the beach on a walk. Sometimes you just couldn't figure out guys no matter how hard you tried.

"I can't believe you get to do this every day," I said. I gazed around the harbor at the various sailboats that were moored and a few bigger boats that were heading out to sea. There was a large saltwater pond, where Claire and I were sailing in one of the small Sunfish-type boats the Inn used with the kids.

"Sure, but it's not always fun," Claire said. "Remember that. I usually have a boat full of eight-year-olds who don't really know what they're doing, but they insist on doing everything."

"How many times have you tipped over?"

"None, so far. But that's only because I watch them so carefully. If I ever lose my concentration, forget about it. We'll be swimming. So what did you do this morning?"

I told her about working at the breakfast place, the tip from C. Q., and the conversation

I'd had—or hadn't had—with Hayden earlier.

"The guy thinks he owns the Inn. Forget him," Claire said. "I mean, if you want to ruin your summer, then okay, go after him."

"I wasn't going after him," I said. "Really. I just—I don't get it when people act one way in public and another in private."

"It's called being two-faced. Come on. He can't be the first person you've met like that," she said.

"I don't know. Maybe he is," I said.

"You're lucky then. I can think of a dozen people in my homeroom like that."

I laughed. "Seriously?"

"Oh yeah. They'd be really sweet to you, if they needed something. If not . . . well, forget it."

"Yeah, I guess I know people like that."

"So then the question is, what does Hayden need from you?"

"Other than my hot body and sparkling wit?" I joked. "Hm, let's think."

"I think he has to make out with all the new girls," Claire said.

"What?" I laughed for a second, but then stopped. It seemed kind of horribly possible. "Has he made a move on you?" I asked Claire.

"No, he's obviously starting with the easy conquests, like you, then working up to the more difficult ones, like me—"

"You are so about to go over for the first time," I threatened, laughing.

"You don't even know how to sail—"

"No, but I do know you need this!" I was about to take out the centerboard when my phone rang. I pulled my phone out of my shorts pocket, thinking that I probably shouldn't have brought my phone out on the sailboat. If we tipped over, good-bye phone.

"If that's Miss Crossley, tell her you're horribly busy," Claire said. "Tell her you're drowning."

"No, it's not her—she always uses the pager. I don't know who it is," I said, flipping open my phone. "Hello?"

"Hey, Lize. Where are you?"

"Josh? No. Hayden?" I said. "That you?" It's always weird when someone calls you for the first time and you don't recognize their phone voice.

Claire looked up from the rudder she'd been adjusting.

"Yeah, it's me," Hayden said.

"How did you get this number?" I asked.

"What, is it off-limits? I got it from the employee list. Anyway, I was thinking maybe we could meet up and go for a bike ride later," Hayden said.

"A bike ride. On the handlebars again?" I smiled at the memory of Hayden and I tottering along the oceanside road, hurrying back to the Inn.

"Well, yeah, that'd be fun. But I don't know if we could go more than a mile without crashing," Hayden said.

"True," I agreed. "Good point."

"No, I have a bike for you, from the shed."

"So a bike ride." I glanced over at Claire and mouthed, *What should I do?*

She didn't say anything, but she didn't have to. I knew what she was thinking: Go slowly. Be careful. Don't do something stupid.

"Well, I'm kind of busy. Right now.

Actually," I said, "Claire and I are sailing. More like she's sailing, and I'm learning."

"I was talking about later this afternoon," he said. "Maybe after dinner—that'd be cool, right? We'd have more time, we could take off for a while."

"Oh. Well, I think I'm going to be busy then, too," I said.

"Really."

"Yeah. You won't believe what Miss Crossley has me doing." *Think fast, Liza. Think of some outlandish errand you're going to be on.*

"What?"

"It's for that writer. I have to, uh, do a bunch of errands for him. He wants to experience the authentic coastal . . . experience, so I'm actually driving him around the area, showing him the local hot spots. I guess he wants to experience the ultimate local seafood takeout or something."

"So where are you taking him?" Hayden asked.

"Uh, I'm not sure yet. But we're leaving around six. Maybe tomorrow—oops—sorry, the boat is tipping—whoa! Gotta go!" I hung up the phone after knocking it against the deck a few times, for maximum effect.

Claire was smiling at me when I looked at her. "Wow. That was some good improv. Your story kind of sucked, but I doubt he'll figure it out. Unless he checks the parking lot for your car . . ."

"So you and I will go for takeout," I said. "Big deal."

"Hey, great idea! No more scullery meals for us."

It felt kind of good, actually. If Hayden could blow me off, like he did earlier, then I could return the favor.

Maybe it only meant I was playing games with him, that I was playing hard to get.

But *shouldn't* I be hard to get?

Shouldn't everybody?

Chapter Nine

Be careful what you wish for. It just might come true.

Those words kept echoing in my head. The night before, I'd tried to come up with some ridiculous task for Miss Crossley to send me on, and I'd invented a story.

Then she came up with something more heinous and involved than I ever could have imagined. I was stuck in her office, catching up on months of filing.

Filing. On one of the nicest days of the entire summer,

I'd started the night before and so far, had been working all morning on it. I couldn't imagine Miss Crossley, as organized as she was, getting this far behind on anything in her life. She tried to tell me it wasn't her fault, that the files actually belonged to the Talbots, but I wasn't sure I believed her. She could be one of those people who seems really put together . . . and then you ride in their car, and there's junk everywhere, like change on the floor, and old fast-food bags, and random notebook pages, and dried-up shriveled French fries.

Anyway, let's just say that *someone* hadn't kept up with the files over the winter. Or the summer before that. Or the entire decade before that.

I'd been crouched on the floor for a long time, so I stood up to stretch my arms over my head. Then I went to the window behind Miss Crossley's desk and looked out at the ocean.

There must have been a storm out at sea the night before—it had rained buckets here onshore—because the waves rolling in looked bigger than usual. I wondered if the swimming was dangerous—or just fun. I loved bodysurfing on days with big surf. Maybe Hayden had his hands full today. But I didn't want to think about him, necessarily. If I started to think of him that way, as someone I was interested in,

I would end up ruining my summer. He obviously had some kind of issue, or at least he did yesterday at the beach. Maybe he was only moody, I thought. Of all the times he'd talked with me, he'd only been rude that one time. So maybe he deserved the chance to explain himself before I wrote him off completely.

"Excuse me, but what are you doing here?"

I turned from the window and saw Mr. "Uptight" Knight, my one-day housekeeping supervisor, standing in the doorway.

"I'm organizing and cleaning the office," I said.

Mr. Knight raised his eyebrows. "You are? *You?*"

"I'm very organized," I said.

"Yes, well, as long as there aren't any belts to be filed, I suppose you'll do a fine job."

Boy. You ruin someone's belt and some people never forgive you. It wasn't even *that* nice of a belt, even if it was designer, and even if it cost two hundred dollars, like the guest claimed. Personally I think he was just looking to make some easy money.

"Miss Crossley does know you're doing this, doesn't she?" he asked.

Was he joking? "Do you think I'm doing this on my own? For fun?" I replied.

"No, I'm just surprised." He straightened his tie. "She could have asked someone on my team."

I decided I should try to get on Mr. Knight's good side. Maybe he was on the outs, the least-favorite cousin, but he was still in the Talbot family. "Yes, but your, ah, clean team members are all busy doing something more important," I said. "Keeping the guests happy. This is a lower priority."

"And that's where you come in," Mr. Knight said.

"Uh . . . yes." Did he have to make me sound so awful? "I'm the Inn gofer. Like a temp. Wherever they need me, that's where I am. So this type of thing is the perfect project for me. Besides, I've been an office manager before."

"You have?"

I nodded as I slid some red hanging files

into the cabinet. I didn't tell him that the office I supposedly managed was my mother's home office. And that I'd done it under duress, because I owed her some money, and that was the solution she came up with for me to pay it back. "Sure, I've been an office manager. I've done lots of this kind of stuff before—typing, filing, answering the phone—"

"Everything but vacuuming," Mr. Knight said.

"Yes, that's my motto, actually," I joked.

He looked at me as though I'd crossed some invisible line of good taste. Still too soon to joke about the demise of the Hulk, I guessed.

Freedom! Sun! Outdoors!

I didn't yell it out loud, but I could have as I ran back to the dorm to change into my swimsuit. Miss Crossley had told me I'd be free for a couple of hours, unless something she didn't anticipate came up. Which it probably would, so I was rushing—she had to give me a half hour anyway, because I was pretty sure that was the law. I left my pager on my dresser and then I practically sprinted from the dorm down to the beach.

I saw Hayden sitting atop his lifeguard chair and I really wanted to go talk to him, but I kept running. I sprinted into the ocean and dove under an incoming wave. I felt the cold water engulf me, the wave roiling the sand beneath me.

When I finally surfaced, I noticed something strange.

I seemed to be the only one in the ocean. As far as I could see, anyway. But then, it was almost lunchtime, and the place tended to clear out right around then—people headed in to take a break from the midday sun, or else they ate lunch and napped under big umbrellas.

I heard a loud shrieking whistle and looked back toward shore. Hayden was standing on the beach, his arms on his hips, a whistle to his lips. He blew the whistle again and waved his arms in the air.

Boy. He really wanted my attention. Maybe I wasn't wrong to think he was interested in me.

I swam back toward shore, catching one

of the smaller waves and riding the crest of it to move along faster, since he looked a bit desperate. You know, some guys are like that, I thought. All you have to do is reject them once, and they decide they have to have you. Typical.

I stood up, leaned back to dunk my hair underwater, then strode out of the surf toward him. "Hey, what's—"

"Did you *not* see the caution flag?" he asked.

"What caution flag?"

"Right there." He pointed to a red, diagonal flag flapping in the breeze directly above his lifeguard stand. "It means no swimming."

"Oh. Whoops. I'm sorry." I looked up and down the beach. The water was definitely clear of people. They were all sitting under umbrellas, or lying in the sun, or playing Frisbee or volleyball. Definitely no swimming going on.

"Do you always break the rules?" Hayden asked.

"Ha!" I laughed. "No. Not *always.*"

"Seriously," he said, with a frown to let me know he meant it.

"Seriously? Do I have to?"

"Have to what?"

"Be so serious. I've been stuck inside all morning, being *extremely* serious about cleaning and picking up and organizing and—after a while I just wanted to throw all the files out the window and watch them blow away in the wind."

Hayden looked at me as if I were going insane. And maybe I had gotten a little too much cabin fever. "What files?" he asked.

"Inn files. Since the year 1900. Miss Crossley couldn't find anything else for me to do, so she roped me into this huge straightening and tidying project." I groaned. "I started last night, actually."

"Hm. Funny. About last night. Weren't you taking that writer on a tour?"

"Oh, yeah. I was." Whoops. "After that, I mean."

"So, would that have been before or after I saw you and Claire shrieking and running into the dorm in the middle of that downpour around seven o'clock?" Hayden asked.

He was quite the detective, wasn't he? Why

was I so stupid? "Why? Where were you?" I said.

"In my room. It's on the floor below yours, remember?"

I coughed. "Well, good thing we didn't go on that bike ride. I mean, really. We'd have gotten drenched."

Hayden folded his arms across his chest and stared at me. "Why did you make up an excuse not to go? I mean, if you don't want to hang with me, then don't, and just say that. It's not like I won't be able to *live* with that."

His tone was suddenly not so carefree and happy. He didn't even sound like the guy I kind of, sort of, knew.

Plus, I didn't like the implication that he could live after being rejected by me. Maybe it was true, but I liked to think of guys slowly falling apart after I turned them down.

"Me? It's not that I didn't want to hang out with you," I said. "Did I say that? No. Why would I?"

"I don't know. But admit it, you made up some convoluted story, instead of telling me you didn't want to hang out."

I thought about it for a second. I could lie, but what would be the point? "Maybe I did," I said.

"Okay, so I *was* right." He smiled, as if winning the argument was important.

"And you're excited that I did this? You're thrilled to be dissed?"

"Did I say that?" He laughed. "I just don't get it. Why did you do that?"

"Why did I? Because! You were so rude to me when I came out here to talk to you. I had twenty bucks to share with you. Plus the writer wrote this really cool note, and you could not have cared less. You didn't even talk to me."

"Maybe I had a lot on my mind."

"Sure," I said.

"What? You don't believe me?"

"I don't know. Should I?" I asked.

"Is it totally impossible that I would have a lot on my mind? What, you think my life is easy or something?"

"Well . . . isn't it?" I asked.

"No," he said.

"Hm. Well, maybe you were, um, distracted.

But if you were, it seems like it had a lot more to do with all the people hanging around."

"Exactly. All the people hanging around, in the ocean, swimming," he said. "You think I can just take my eyes off the water because you want me to?"

Well, didn't you, all those other times? I thought. *At least for a second or two?* "You didn't have to look at me—just talk to me," I said. "Anyway, aren't you doing that now?"

"No one's swimming now," he reminded me.

"Oh. Right." I realized with a shiver that I'd gotten really cold, standing there talking to him. The sun had gone behind a cloud, and my skin was covered with goosebumps. "Except that person over there." I pointed to an older man who was just beyond where the waves broke, doing a strong, sustained crawl motion.

"Oh, crap, that's Mr. Anderson," Hayden muttered, and he took off in a jog.

I grabbed my towel and wrapped it around my body, then I turned around and quickly made my way over the hot sand back to the boardwalk. The caution flag should have been up for that, I thought. Hot sand that will burn your feet — make it an orange flag, with red raging hot shooting flames painted on it.

And also maybe a caution flag for Hayden. Stay away. Trouble. They could show a guy in sunglasses with his nose covered in white zinc oxide, a big red X over his face.

Chapter Ten

"*E*xcuse me. Excuse me. Miss?"

Claire and I stopped halfway up the Inn porch steps. A couple was standing to our right. "Yes?" I asked.

"Would you be able to take a picture of me and my wife?" the man asked.

"Sure, no problem." I took the digital camera he offered and snapped several shots of the two of them, leaning against the banister. They looked like they might be wedding guests, all dressed up for the fancy evening ahead.

It was a Wedding Saturday—the first one I would experience at the Inn. The Inn was rented out for weddings almost every Saturday throughout the summer, and some Sundays, too. They were rumored to be very fun, because nearly everyone on staff worked at them.

So, instead of teaching sailing, Claire was going to be serving dinner plates, while I would circulate with trays of appetizers and champagne. It was an "all hands on deck" situation, as Miss Crossley phrased it.

In other words, the Inn catered the wedding and hired cheap help—namely, us—to pull it off.

The dining room had been completely transformed, with elegant tablecloth fabrics, fancy decorations, flowers draped on every surface possible, streamers hung from the ceiling, and a three-tier cake on a table in the center of the room. The room was quickly filling with guests filing in from outside, where the wedding had been performed on the grassy lawn overlooking the ocean.

I couldn't imagine a cooler place to have a wedding than here, right beside the ocean, in a classic place like this. Not that I was thinking wedding thoughts for myself, at least not for another ten years. Hopefully the Inn would still be in business then, and hopefully my to-be-determined-at-a-later-date (or *on* a later date) fiancé would agree that this was the place we wanted to marry. And if he didn't, I'd *make* him agree.

And that attitude, according to my mother, meant that I wasn't even close to being ready for marriage. Which was okay with me.

Claire and I went into the kitchen—I'd only been in the main kitchen a few times—and I was really impressed by what a massive operation the place was. I left Claire and headed to find the person in charge of appetizers. Miss Crossley was, naturally, in the center of everything, giving orders, filling trays, and sending people out to circulate with them, so I stepped up and got mine.

I made my way around the dining room and out on the porch, offering shrimp puffs. I went back to the kitchen and got a new tray, this one with tiny crab cakes. Then I was recruited to help fill water glasses, and then I was carrying trays of entrees out to the dining room and holding them while others served from them, and then I was summoned to carry pieces of cake to everyone after the bride and groom cut the wedding cake.

I was starting to wonder why everyone thought these wedding events were so much fun. I'd never worked so hard in my life. I felt like one of those Sherpas who works in the mountains, carrying everything. Okay, so maybe it wasn't *that* difficult, but still.

The first chance I had to catch my breath was when the bride and groom had their first dance. A lot of the staff were milling about in the kitchen. I started to walk outside, thinking I'd get a breath of fresh air on the porch, if it wasn't too crowded with wedding guests.

But before I got there, I saw C. Q. Wallace leaning against the open dining room doorway, looking in at the reception. "Weddings. What a waste of time," he said to me as I went past.

I stopped and looked at him. He was a curmudgeon, all right, through and through. "What did you say? What are you talking about?"

"Fifty percent of all marriages end in divorce,

yet people still persist in having these expensive, elaborate weddings." He shook his head. "It's a gamble, if you ask me." He rubbed his glasses on the sleeve of his jacket, which he was wearing with a T-shirt, tattered jeans, and flip-flops.

"Are you married?" I asked.

He coughed. "No. Came close a few times, but thankfully, no. I was left at the altar once. Does that count?"

Bitter, party of one, I thought. "Right. Well, if you ask me, who wouldn't want to have a big party when they get married?" I asked.

"And I suppose you're going to tell me that this marriage is going to last, that they're fabulous together, yadda yadda yadda."

"No. I don't even know them," I said, glancing in at the bride and groom, who were dancing with the members of the wedding party.

"Oh." He laughed. "Well, sure, why would you?"

"But I'd say they picked a great place to get married, so they're off to a pretty good start," I said. I remembered something he'd told me when we first met. "Speaking of places. You're still here."

"Thanks for noticing."

I laughed. "No, I mean—you must be getting some writing done, or you would have left by now. So . . . are you?"

"Scads," he said, his voice heavy with sarcasm. "No, not scads—but some. I like how laid-back this place is, during the week. This weekend wedding stuff isn't exactly for me, so I'm heading up to my room for some peace and quiet." He started to walk away, but then he turned back toward me. "Listen. You're the Inn gofer, right? That's what Miss Crossley called you. Horrible name, not to mention it's a rodent, and you're a girl, but as the official Inn gofer—do you think you could score me a piece of wedding cake?"

"Sure." I smiled. "No problem. But wouldn't that kind of be saying you approve of the wedding?"

"No, it just says I like cake and I'm opportunistic," he said. "I'd go in and get it myself, but I'm not really dressed for a wedding."

"It's okay—I've been wanting a piece myself. Be right back," I promised.

I walked into the dining room and grabbed two paper plates with generous-size pieces of cake—I had to take one with a blue rose frosting, because in my family getting one of the flowers on a cake is considered good luck. We usually fight over them at weddings and other events, which is kind of funny.

I was in the back hallway heading toward the stairs with the plates of cake when Hayden stepped out of the business center, in front of me, and blocked my path. "Cake for me? How thoughtful." Hayden took the plate in my left hand.

"Actually, that's for—"

"But let's dance first, I love this song." He took the other plate from me and set both of them on a chair by the window.

I hadn't even seen him working, but he was dressed in black and white like the rest of us. "Where have you been all day?" I asked.

"Valet parking," he said as he lifted my hands to his shoulders. He put his hands on my waist and pulled me close. "I was done for a while so I came in to check e-mail," he said.

"I thought this event was supposed to be all hands on deck, not all hands on Liza," I said, trying to fight how much I was enjoying being this close to him.

Hayden laughed. "Sorry. So what were we even arguing about?"

"You know what," I said. "You totally blew me off."

"Me? You're the one who made up some wacky story just to avoid seeing me," Hayden argued as we danced back and forth in the hallway.

"I'm sorry. That was dumb, but I was trying to get back at you," I said.

"You did. You retaliated, and now we're even."

"So let's start over," I said.

"Okay," Hayden agreed. "We'll start over." We danced in the hallway, barely moving to a slow song. I felt myself kind of getting lost in the moment. "What are we starting over?" he asked after another minute went by. He took a strand of hair that had fallen out of my ponytail and tucked it back behind my ear.

"I don't know," I said, a little breathless. "This?" And I closed my eyes and was about to kiss him when there was this loud ringing in my ears, like the bell that signaled the end of a boxing round. And like two boxers in a clutch, Hayden and I slowly separated.

Miss Crossley was holding the silver bell from the front desk in her palm. "You're needed at the front desk, Liza," she said briskly. "Caroline isn't feeling well and has retired for the evening."

"Too much champagne again?" Hayden joked.

"Hayden, I believe some wedding guests are in need of their car keys," she said.

"I'm on it," he said, and he literally sprinted away down the hall.

"Don't I need to be trained to work at the front desk?" I asked Miss Crossley as she led me through the lobby.

"We'll go over a few things," she promised. "It should be no problem for a person of average intelligence."

She could be so warm sometimes.

C. Q. Wallace stopped by the desk just as I took over. "Never got that piece of cake," he commented.

"No. Sorry. I got, um, redirected," I said.

"Well, gophers have a habit of losing their way. It's a trait of the species."

"Really?" I asked.

"No. The opposite, actually. They build elaborate tunnels. That's how they became known as pests. And they like to be alone, one per tunnel. Which doesn't bode well for your love life."

I felt my face start to turn red when he said that. Love life. Did I have one, or not? *What are we starting over?* Hayden had asked.

"Why do you know so much about gophers?" I asked.

"I'll do anything to procrastinate. I read entire books on weird subjects." He smiled. "So, any chance at all of getting some cake around here?"

"If I can't find any left-over wedding cake?

We'll have a cake baked for you," I promised as I stood up.

Miss Crossley returned just in time to overhear me. She leaned over and whispered in my ear, "You're finally getting the hang of this."

Chapter Eleven

"*W*e should have more days off," Josh said as we pulled back into the parking lot.

"Yeah, and more money to do things with on our days off," Claire added.

Miraculously my car had worked well that day, starting after only a few attempts, and it hadn't stranded us on the side of the road. We'd taken a trip to see Newport, and it was kind of funny to see my beaten-up, rusted, dented old car parked among the expensive BMWs and Mercedes.

"Can you believe some of those mansions?" Josh asked. "I mean, if you lived there, you wouldn't even ever see your family."

"No," Claire said, "just the butler, maid, and any other servants—"

"Who all come from the scullery," Josh added, and we all laughed as we climbed out of the car. "Like us."

Caroline was walking out of the dorm, and she stopped in the small parking lot. "Where have *you* been?" She looked at my car as if it might contaminate her air space.

"Newport. You know, slumming. The *new* people have to go to *New*port," Josh said to Caroline.

"Ha ha," she said. "Very funny."

Josh threw a bag over his shoulder. "I thought so."

"Me too," I added. "So, what did we miss around here?"

"Miss Crossley's been looking for you. All over the place," Caroline said.

I sighed. Couldn't that woman hire another gofer or something? I wasn't the only person who could fill in at the last minute, was I? Wait. Maybe I was. "But it's my day off. She told me I was off on Mondays, because it's the slowest day here."

"She needed you anyway." Caroline made it sound like a desperate situation. "Didn't you take your pager with you?"

"No. If I'm not working, then I'm not working. It wouldn't do her any good to page me if I'm in Newport." I hadn't brought my cell phone, either, but that was because I'd forgotten it.

"If you say so. But I think you have some notes on your door. Don't say I didn't warn you." Caroline headed off down the path in the direction of the Inn.

"Ooh. Intriguing," Josh commented.

"Josh, notes from Miss Crossley aren't intriguing," I said. "They're annoying."

Claire and I headed upstairs to our room. We had a small bulletin board on our door, and there was a big yellow Post-it that said, "LIZA MCKENZIE," on it. As if there were other Lizas in this room that might be confused. I turned the note over and read Miss Crossley's note: "Ignore all earlier messages. Problem solved!" And there was a little smiley face drawn at the bottom.

"A smiley face? Since when is Miss Crossley a smiley-face type of person?" I asked Claire.

I plowed through the other notes from her.

It was amazing how many times she'd come by in the six or seven hours we'd been gone.

The last note was in different handwriting that I didn't recognize, and jotted on an old envelope instead of a Post-it.

> Where are you? We need to make a
> pen run tonight.
> Meet me at the Shuttle at 6:30.
> H

"I can't believe he changed his pen brand. How crazy is that?" Hayden asked.

We were walking on the beach. Our jeans were rolled up at the bottom and we walked barefoot on the hard sand just above where the waves washed ashore. It was a cool evening, and kind of breezy.

We'd taken guests with us to the train, and brought new ones back as well, so Hayden and I hadn't really had a chance to visit during the shuttle ride. For once, the train had been on time, so I'd sprinted to the office store and back.

"I guess writers will try anything when they're stuck," I said.

"How many nights has he been staying at the Inn already?"

"A week or two, at least."

"I'd use about *one* pen in that time. What does he do, use one per day?" Hayden asked.

"Yeah, he's tough on the pens. Wears 'em right out. By not writing with them. Go figure." I explained how Mr. Wallace had told me about his writer's block, which I guessed must have been disappearing, since he was sticking around and ordering more pens.

"I thought writers wrote on computers, anyway," Hayden said.

"He uses both, I guess. Hey, if he and Miss Crossley want to send me on these missions, and I get to hang with you, and get a tip from him? It's cool with me."

"Yeah, but what will we do when he checks out? I mean, what's going to be our excuse?" Hayden asked.

"Excuse?"

"To hang, like you said."

"Oh." I smiled nervously. "Maybe another slightly eccentric person with no car and an urgent need for office supplies will check in."

"Yeah, maybe," Hayden said. "Should we count on that, though?"

We walked side by side down the beach. Did we really need an excuse, I wondered, or could we just do this because we wanted to?

Hayden seemed to have slipped into a melancholy mood, so I took his arm and linked it through mine. "Everything okay?" I asked.

He shrugged. "Yeah."

"You sure?"

"No."

"Why? What's going on?"

"Just thinking about stuff. My family. I talked to my mom today. And, see, she and my dad . . . my parents are getting separated," Hayden said. "They just announced this like right before I was leaving for the summer."

"Oh, no. I'm sorry. That's hard."

"Yeah, it is. And my little sister—she's gone goth or something to protest."

"That's not the end of the world," I said.

"Yeah. But you don't know my sister. She was always really into girly girl stuff. Anyway, *she* called me today, begging me to come home for the summer because she hates both Mom and Dad," Hayden said. "Which I can't do, but I wish I could for her sake."

"Maybe she could come here to visit," I suggested.

"Maybe, but she wouldn't want to hang out with either my mom or dad long enough to drive here," Hayden said with a laugh. "She used to love it here. But now she hates the beach, the sun, anything not goth."

"It's a phase. Don't worry about it," I told him. "Hey, even I was goth once."

"You?"

"Sure. I wore all black, I wore dark lipstick, dyed my hair black . . ."

"And what happened?"

"I got bored. I kind of get bored quickly," I said. "Especially with hair. So when did you start vacationing here? What's your connection to this place?"

"Well, we used to come to the Inn when I was a little kid—like, very little."

"You were little once? No."

Hayden pushed me toward the surf, and my ankles got wet. "You're pretty tall yourself. How tall?"

"Five eight and a half," I said. "So tell me about your family some more. You have a little sister—any other siblings?"

"I have an older brother. He worked here for three summers, and that's how I got in," Hayden explained. "That's my connection. How about you?"

"This is kind of funny, but my grandfather knows Mr. Talbot Senior, from way back when. But even so, I got hired at the last minute," I explained. "And I tried to get hired last year, too."

"Don't take it personally. Everyone wants to come back, so there are only like five or six new slots a summer. And if you factor in all the people the Talbots know personally, or owe favors to . . . and then there are the people like me, whose siblings worked here, and unless *they* royally screwed up, then the Talbots reward them by giving a spot to their brother or sister."

"Yeah. Claire's sister worked here," I told him.

"So I'm guessing you don't have an older sister to get you in."

"Why? Did you want to meet her?" I teased him.

"*No*, I'm just trying to ask about your family," Hayden said.

"I'm an only child. I was one of those extremely difficult babies, so my parents decided to stop after me."

"No, come on. You're not *that* difficult."

"What? Shut up." I pushed him up the beach, and he stumbled on a couple of shells.

"Ow," he said, brushing a sharp piece off his foot. "Maybe you are." He looked up at the sky for a second, and I stopped walking to stand beside him. "We should probably turn around and go back," Hayden said.

"Probably," I said.

"It's getting late. We're lucky the moon is so bright tonight, or we wouldn't be able to see a thing."

I gazed at the moon, which wasn't exactly

full, but was close. There was something really romantic about only seeing by the light of the moon, while letting the ocean's water roll over your feet.

"Feel like swimming?" Hayden asked.

"No, not tonight. It's kind of chilly for that," I said.

"Then let's sit down for a second and just listen to the water," he said.

"You like doing that, too? I used to drive my parents crazy by insisting on doing that. Plus I used to make them open all the car windows or else stop the car when we got within range of salt air, just so I could inhale it."

"But . . . weren't you coming toward the ocean?" Hayden sounded confused.

"Yes."

"So you'd be smelling the salt air for days, wouldn't you?" Hayden asked.

"Right. Sure, but that's nothing like the first *breaths* of it," I argued.

"Clearly you need to move."

"Clearly."

Hayden folded up his sweatshirt and made

a pillow for both of us, and we lay back in the sand, next to each other.

"You should be a travel agent," Hayden said. "Or wait—no, you should be in advertising. You should write about this stuff."

"You think?" I asked.

It felt so natural to be with him like this, but at the same time it also felt wrong because I hadn't been completely honest. *You have to tell him about Mark,* I thought. But why did I have to? Mark was a nonissue. Though I could just see him saying, "You called me a 'nonissue'? Thanks a lot!"

"What do you want to do, you know, with your life?" Hayden asked.

"I'm not sure. Isn't that terrible? I should know. I'm going to college, you know?" I said. "What about you?"

"College sophomore."

"So, what's your major then?" I asked.

"I started in business. Hated it. Then I switched to chemistry. Hated it. So I don't know." He laughed. "I guess I can fall back on lifeguarding, until I'm like twenty-five. After that it won't be cool anymore."

"Yeah, gray hair and lifeguards don't really match," I said.

"No?" Hayden turned over onto his side to face me. He started to play with my hair, and I stared up at the stars above us. I really, really wanted to turn toward him and kiss him, but now that I'd thought of Mark, I knew that I couldn't, not until I was honest with Hayden.

"Listen, there's something I have to tell you," I said.

"Uh oh. That sounds bad."

"No, it's not bad. It's just—remember when you asked if I was seeing someone? And I said, no, because I'm not. But I did have a boyfriend before I came here."

"Stashed under the bed, like I said."

I laughed. "No, more like working at a factory making boat parts. We're on a break for the summer. Probably longer, actually."

"Summer break, huh? I haven't heard of that. Well, did you guys agree that you can see other people?"

"The way we left it, we weren't all that . . . clear. Or mature." I laughed. "It was more like an argument. He said that if I came here I could forget about him for the summer. And I said fine, done, and I packed up and here I am. And we haven't spoken since. I mean, how could he be against anyone wanting to come here? It's like heaven here, you know?"

"You miss him?"

"Not yet. Not really at all, actually." Now that I thought about it, that was kind of strange. I guessed maybe we'd been ready to move on for a while, if I was willing to leave him for the summer and he was willing to let me go. "Anyway, it's pretty much over," I said. "But we haven't had that final conversation, so it's not over, over."

"I used to order my eggs like that. Over over," Hayden said.

I smiled. "Thanks for having a sense of humor about this." This conversation could have gone much, much worse, I thought, considering I could have—and probably should have—shared this with him days ago.

Hayden held up his watch and pressed a button to light its face. 11:54. "It really is late—we should go."

We had a basic, but not all that enforced,

curfew of midnight. We both got to our feet and jogged back the way we'd come, without talking much. When we got back to the Inn, Hayden turned to head that way instead of up the path to the dorm.

"You know what? I left some stuff at the Inn I need to grab," he said.

"I can wait for you," I offered.

"No, it's okay—you go ahead. I'll see you tomorrow," he said.

I let him go and didn't argue the point. I didn't want the night to end, but okay, maybe things were moving a little too quickly for both of us, especially considering I'd just sort of dropped a bombshell.

We didn't kiss good night, which was okay because I was still feeling weird about doing something with someone else without talking to Mark first.

"Where were you?" Claire asked when I walked into our room. She was sitting up in bed, reading one of the nonfun books she'd brought along. "You almost missed curfew."

"I was with Hayden," I said softly. I didn't want Zoe and especially Caroline next door to hear. I didn't want anyone else to figure out what was going on until I had at least figured it out for myself. I could picture Caroline with her ear pressed to the wall, just praying for some good gossip.

"What did you guys do? Or shouldn't I ask?" Claire said.

"Nothing. We went for a walk and we just talked about . . . everything," I said.

"Really. But it's past midnight," she said.

"I know. But I'm completely serious. Nothing happened."

"Remember, this place will get really small if you and Hayden . . . you know."

"I know," I said.

But the truth was, I could handle whatever came at me. I wasn't scared. Maybe I should have been, but I wasn't.

Or maybe some things were worth being scared to death about—and following through anyway.

Chapter Twelve

*T*he next night, there was a party at Crandall's Point. It was sort of impromptu in that no one told me and Claire about it. So, according to us, impromptu now meant "last minute, and you're not invited."

"The dorm is so quiet tonight. What's up with that?" Claire had asked me around 8:00.

"It's like everyone went somewhere, without us," I commented.

Then she vaguely remembered Josh saying something about a party. But why hadn't Hayden?

We headed out to Crandall's Point, and when we came over the crest of a sand dune, I saw two figures standing off to the side, behind everyone else. It looked like a guy and girl, so

I was wondering who had hooked up—they were standing really close.

As we got nearer to them, I realized: It was Hayden. And Zoe. They were sort of huddled together against a big rock, as if they were shielding themselves from the wind. But there was no wind. Still, I felt a cold ripple down the back of my neck when I saw them. They had this look as if they were conspiring. They didn't even see us, so I slunk away feeling like I'd intruded on a private moment.

If Hayden and Zoe were still "close," as Caroline had so nicely phrased it, why hadn't he told me the night before, when I'd come clean about Mark? It wasn't like he hadn't had the perfect opportunity.

Did he not tell me about the party because he knew Zoe would be there? But that didn't make sense—they could be around each other tons, back at the Inn or the dorm. They didn't need a secret party to get together. Besides, she was seeing Brandon. Wasn't she?

Claire tugged at my arm to make me keep walking, because I was a little frozen in place, reluctant to proceed. "It's probably just one of those post-breakup talks you have to have," she suggested.

"What are those?" I asked.

Claire shrugged. "How would I know? I've never had one. I've never dated anyone more than once."

"Once? What do you mean?"

"To a movie or a party or whatever." Claire grabbed a soda from a cooler and opened it. "Just never seemed worth it before now."

"Before now?"

"Before we go to college, I mean. Because you'll change so much. My sister said high school guys aren't worth it, anyway."

I looked at her for a few seconds. "I think you need to stop getting all your guy advice from your big sister. She sounds a little jaded."

Claire laughed. "You have a point."

"What took you guys so long?" Josh asked when we sat down beside him. "I was wondering where you were."

"You were?" Claire asked, sounding surprised.

"Well, yeah."

"We didn't know this was where everyone was," I said. *Because certain people didn't share information with certain other people. Because they are off having deep discussions with their supposedly ex-girlfriends.*

"Well, where else would we be?" Caroline said. "It's not like there are multiple hangouts to choose from."

"Sure there are," I said. "You just haven't thought of them all. You're stuck in a rut."

Just then, I noticed Hayden walking over to the group. Zoe wasn't with him, which seemed strange. What had happened? He sat across the fire from us. I thought he might sit next to me, or at least maybe make a point of saying hi, but he didn't. I tried to catch his eye and wave at him, but it was like he was deliberately avoiding me. What had I done? Was this all about the Mark thing?

"Did Zoe take off?" Caroline asked him.

Leave it to her to find out the dirt, but this time I was grateful—she saved me from asking the question and looking desperate.

"Brandon picked her up," Hayden said.

"Didn't you hear his Harley? We heard this loud exhaust roar out on the street, and she bolted."

Bolted because she was about to be caught with you? I wondered. *Or bolted, in general, because she's skittish, like a horse?*

Except she wasn't skittish, at all.

"The neighbors freaked. The Crandalls will be down momentarily to kick us all off their point," Hayden joked. "They're taking back their rocks."

"Is there a law against Harleys?" Josh asked.

"There should be," Caroline said with a frown.

"Don't you approve of Brandon?" Claire asked her.

"No, but I mean, it's not up to me." Caroline shrugged.

"And thank you, Caroline," Hayden said. "I'm sure Zoe appreciates you butting out of her life."

Caroline gave him a very huffy look. "I think she could do better, and so do her parents, but whatever."

I glanced across the bonfire ring at Hayden,

but he didn't make eye contact. What was he doing, exactly? Were he and Zoe friends, or weren't they?

Everyone including Caroline knew that they went off to talk privately, and they didn't think that was weird. So everyone from last summer must know they still had some sort of connection *this* summer.

So what did that make me, for spending so much time with Hayden and thinking we might have a "thing"? A fool, right?

I was starting to wish we'd never found this supposed party. I definitely didn't feel like sticking around. "I'm going to take off," I said to Claire, who was laughing with Josh about something.

"Want me to go, too?" she asked, looking up at me as I got to my feet.

"No, you stay—I'm exhausted," I said. Which was one word for it. Some others were *confused*, *hurt*, *surprised*, *shocked*, and *baffled*. And I didn't even have a thesaurus with me.

I walked back the way I'd come, picking my way between rocks until I got to the flat sand, and then I moved faster. I almost felt like running, but if I did, and I got back to the dorm too soon, what would I do for the rest of the night? Or should I head to the Inn and look for a guest who needed someone to play backgammon with?

Yes, that was pathetic. But maybe I was pathetic, going after a guy who wasn't really interested if his former girlfriend was around and available. But she was with Brandon, wasn't she? It was really bothering me that I couldn't figure this all out, that the "inn crowd" seemed to know more than I did. The one person who might explain it to me was Caroline, but I couldn't ask her.

I was nearly back to the Inn when I heard footsteps slapping on the sand behind me.

He waited long enough, I thought as I turned around and saw Hayden.

"I have a surprise," he said.

Yeah. I think I already experienced that, I thought. "Really," I said.

"Come on, let's go to the top deck."

"We can't get up there," I said. *Never mind*

the fact that I don't know if I'm even talking to you.

The deck was connected to the Inn's biggest and best room, the honeymoon suite, and could only be used by guests who were staying there or for private parties. I'd never even seen it, not on our tour, because Miss Crossley said it was off-limits.

"The room's not rented tonight. I have a pass key," Hayden said.

I considered my options as we neared the Inn's front entrance. I liked the idea of an adventure with Hayden. I wouldn't mind seeing this famous deck. Plus, if we were going to argue, it would be very private up there—privacy wasn't something we'd have back at the dorm or out here on the porch.

"Okay, sure," I said.

We went inside and pressed the call button for the elevator. When it came, we stepped inside and looked awkwardly at each other. Unfortunately we were the only ones in there. Fortunately it was only four floors to the top. Hayden inserted a special electronic key card that made the elevator stop at the fourth floor.

Once we stepped out, there was a hallway.

There were two doors when we got to the top: one for the honeymoon suite and one for the deck.

"You want to see the suite first?" Hayden asked.

"Not right now," I said. The last place I wanted to be with him was in a romantic room with a giant bed. I'd probably hit him over the head with a flower vase.

I walked outside and went around the edge of the deck, checking out the view. I could hear glasses clinking and people laughing on the front porch of the Inn. One male guest had a really loud, obnoxious laugh—an actual guffaw—and when I heard it, I glanced back over my shoulder at Hayden and we both laughed. I was grateful to the guy for laughing like that, because it broke the tension. Which wasn't to say there wasn't still tension, and a couple of things I wanted to clear up.

"So, when we were back at Crandall's Point?" I began.

"Yeah?" Hayden asked.

"The way you acted toward me, it was like we'd never hung out the night before—or ever," I said.

"What? No, it wasn't," Hayden protested.

"Yeah, it *was*."

"Look. If you want someone who's into PDA, that's not me."

"Well, I'm not into PDR," I said.

"PDR?" Hayden asked.

"Public displays of rejection," I said.

Hayden started to laugh. "That's really a term?"

"Sure," I said.

"It's just awkward, that's all," Hayden said. "People like to talk, and I don't like being talked about."

"What are you so afraid of?" I asked.

"Truthfully? I don't know. Let's talk about something else. I'm starting to sound paranoid."

"Okay." I took a deep breath. I was ready for whatever he had to tell me. "Can we talk about the Zoe thing?"

Hayden looked at me and raised an eyebrow.

"I'm not the jealous type. Really. Honestly

I'm not. But tonight you guys were off having this totally . . . I don't know—"

"That? That was just family stuff. From home. I'll tell you about it sometime. But we're friends, that's all," Hayden said.

I wasn't sure whether I believed him yet.

"I mean, *you* know how it is, after you date someone. You're still a—a close friend, sort of. Aren't you and what's-his-name still friends?"

"I don't know. We haven't talked," I said. "So probably no. But okay, I take your point, I guess."

"So can we officially move on?" he asked.

I couldn't see why not, even if it felt a little strange. "Sure."

"Good." Hayden put his arms around my waist. "Isn't it great up here?"

"Yeah." I leaned back against him, enjoying the feeling of being close to him. We fit together perfectly. From the upstairs deck you could see everything around the Inn, the entire property, from the dorm to the tennis court to the sailing pond to the ocean beach.

"So how did you end up with a key?" I asked. "Wait, don't tell me. Miss Crossley gave it to you, like the key to the bike shed. You have your special privileges."

"No, actually I just sort of borrowed it for tonight, from the front desk."

"The front *desk*?" I pretended to gasp. "Was Caroline there?"

"She was fawning all over some California dude checking in," Hayden said. "She never even saw me."

I laughed. "You know what? I like this side of you."

"Which side is that?" Hayden let go of me and turned around, stopping to pose and flexing his biceps. "Front side, back side . . ."

I swatted him on the butt. "The daredevil side."

"Yeah. We'll have to be quiet though. If we get busted, we're in big trouble."

"Okay, so we'll quietly listen to the surf," I said.

"Very quietly."

"Definitely." I nodded. We stood there for a few minutes, me leaning back against him again, both of us watching the ocean. I closed my eyes for a while and just listened to the water, the rhythmic rolling sound of the waves.

Hayden gently took my shoulders and turned me so that I was facing him.

"Wasn't I being quiet enough?" I asked in a whisper.

"Too quiet." He traced my cheekbones with his fingers. "I thought maybe you fell asleep."

"No. Not exactly," I said as I looked into his eyes. "You have the coolest eyes. You know that? They're sort of blue, but then they're sort of gray—"

Hayden interrupted me by leaning down to kiss me. I wrapped my arms around his waist, and he pulled me in tight. We must have been kissing for a while, and I was totally lost in the moment. I completely forgot where I was.

Then the outside deck lights came on.

Chapter Thirteen

*W*e jumped apart. If that was Miss Crossley, or anyone on the Inn staff . . . We were so in trouble. We'd already been caught once by her, dancing when we were supposed to be working. If she found us up here? Even her favorite employee, Hayden, would be history.

"You said no one was staying here!" I whispered to him. "What are we going to do?"

I had a brief mental image of the two of us scaling the side of the Inn, like in a heist movie.

"Don't sweat it," Hayden said. "Come on, let's see who it is."

"This feels really, really weird," I said as we edged closer to the sliding glass door and peered into the honeymoon suite. Of all the rooms to *spy* on.

All of a sudden the door opened. Mr. Talbot Junior was standing there.

I opened my mouth to say something, but nothing came out. Not even air, because I'd stopped breathing.

"Hello, Mr. Talbot. Sir," Hayden said.

"Hayden, is that all you have to say? Hello?"

"It's . . . a nice night?" I added.

Mr. Talbot looked at me and his mouth turned into an even deeper frown. "And what is your name again?"

"Liza," I said. "Elizabeth McKenzie." I wished that it was Mr. Talbot Senior, who might actually recognize my name and give me a break.

"Elizabeth McKenzie," he repeated as if trying to memorize my name. "Well, Hayden and Elizabeth. What do you two think you're doing up here?" he asked. "Other than getting to know each other better." He coughed a few times. "Substantially better, I might add."

Hayden looked over at me, and if he wasn't

turning red from embarrassment, then I certainly was.

"Still speechless? Well, imagine my surprise when I walked into the office to deposit some cash and receipts into the safe. There's a surveillance system in the office, and there's a camera trained on this deck when the room is vacant. Or have you forgotten?"

"I suppose, sir, that I did forget," Hayden said. "My apologies."

I should have known, too—I'd only just spent hours cleaning and organizing that office.

"So. What do you have to say for yourselves?" Mr. Talbot demanded.

That we're about to lose our jobs? I thought. *Good-bye, this has been a great place to work?*

"Mr. Talbot, I'm really sorry. I just wanted to show the place to Liza. It's my fault," Hayden said. "I take full responsibility."

"There are two people standing here, so in my opinion, you're both responsible. It's not as if you both don't know the rules." Mr. Talbot glared at me.

"I'm sorry. We definitely shouldn't have

been up here," I said. "It's just—it's such a beautiful spot. We got carried away."

"It is beautiful," Mr. Talbot agreed. "And such a nice night." He took a deep breath and stretched his arms over his head. He seemed to be loosening up a little bit. "I wish I'd been up here, instead of in the office. Then you'd never have been able to get away with this."

I just stood there, smiling and feeling stupid. *Had* we gotten away with it? Or were we about to spend our last night at the Inn?

"I should have checked with you first, Mr. Talbot," Hayden said. "I mean, if I'd thought it through, I would have done that. It was an impulse decision."

"Hayden, I've learned over the years to trust you. And if you'll trust me for a second, let me give you a piece of advice." Mr. Talbot put his hands on the wall and leaned out over the deck. "And that is, never go with an impulsive decision. Never."

Hayden laughed. "I can see where you're right."

"Who said . . . fools rush in—"

"Where angels fear to tread," I said. "Alexander Pope."

Mr. Talbot looked at me with newfound respect. "Very impressive."

"My grandfather," I said. "He's always quoting that." And now I knew *why*. All those years he drove me nuts by saying that, he was trying to warn me for situations like this.

"Look, I realize you probably need to report this to Miss Crossley," Hayden said.

"Probably," Mr. Talbot agreed. "That would be the way we'd usually handle it."

"But if there's any way we could . . . I don't know. I know this is a lot to ask," Hayden said, "but if we could keep this between us, I'd really appreciate it."

Mr. Talbot didn't say anything for a minute or two. He was staring up at the sky. "Look, isn't that the Milky Way?"

"Actually, *that* is." I started to point out different constellations to him. That astronomy minicourse we'd done in school was really coming in handy. Mr. Talbot seemed to have forgotten all about the fact we were only seeing all these stars and constellations because we were standing somewhere we shouldn't be. "It's so amazing here," I commented. "You can see so much more here than back home."

"Light pollution. It's a problem," Mr. Talbot agreed. "That's why I love the Inn's location. That's why city people love to come here."

"You should mention that in the brochure," I said. "Talk about all the open sky and dark nights—"

"And romantic locations?" Mr. Talbot turned back to us. "Well. Hayden, I've been thinking about what you asked. It's asking a lot."

"I know that, sir—"

"But I'm inclined to agree with you. We don't need to share this." Mr. Talbot extended his palm and Hayden placed the key card into it. "Now, I should get back to the office, and you should get back to the dorm. And don't make any more stops on the way."

When we got back downstairs, Mr. Talbot headed for the office. Hayden and I looked at each other and I let out a big sigh.

"I think I'm going to go see if he, uh, needs any help," Hayden said.

"Sounds good," I said. For some reason I just wanted to get out of there.

We quickly went our separate ways without even saying anything else, like "good night," or "it was nice kissing you." I think we were both sort of in shock from everything that had just happened.

Then I ran back to the dorm and, of course, told Claire everything.

I mean, what are roommates for?

The next morning we were all eating breakfast when Miss Crossley walked into the Hull. Trailing her were all the employees from the restaurant upstairs, and everyone else currently on duty and in uniform.

"Are we having a meeting?" Brooke asked.

"I didn't know we were having a meeting," Caroline said.

Miss Crossley banged a knife against a glass to get everyone's attention. Not that everyone hadn't stopped talking when she walked in, because she looked so serious and because the wait staff didn't often leave work to follow her around.

"I'll make this quick, everyone. We're letting someone go, and you need to hear it from me," Miss Crossley said.

Chapter Fourteen

*M*y last bite of wheat toast stuck in my throat. I gulped and attempted to swallow.

It was obvious what was about to happen. Once the effect of star-gazing wore off, Mr. Talbot had come to his senses and realized Hayden and I should be fired.

I tried to catch Hayden's eye, across the room, but he seemed to be deliberately avoiding me. That was probably a good idea, given the situation. Not that it would help, if Miss Crossley's mind was made up.

Suddenly I noticed that Miss Crossley didn't have her usual pressed-and-starched appearance. She looked a little overwhelmed as she rubbed the side of her face. "I've been up all night deliberating," she said. "It pains me to have to say this."

I chewed my thumbnail. The only person it could truly pain her to fire — would be Hayden. Her favorite, long-time employee. Me, she couldn't care less about, although in her eyes I'd already given her a little bit of trouble. And, as she'd promised that day on the beach, she was watching me extra carefully.

"Something happened last night," Miss Crossley went on.

I started to picture what it would be like to go home after only a few weeks here. How many people I'd run into, around town, and how stupid I'd feel explaining. "I got fired because I was making out with this guy." How lame was that? Why would I risk my job over someone I barely knew? I was an idiot. Pure and simple. This was a good reason *not* to fall in love. You did stupid things.

"An unauthorized Inn employee borrowed the van late last night, which is, bottom line, inexcusable."

I looked up at Miss Crossley. I felt like I'd

just surfaced from being underwater. She was still talking, and she was saying that I wasn't fired. Hayden wasn't fired.

But Tyler was.

"Now, no harm was done. He didn't go on a joyride, or get pulled over for speeding, or anything like that. And he was trying to help out a guest, by taking her to a convenience store on the other side of town. He was finishing his server shift around eleven o'clock, when she apparently settled her bar bill and asked for the trip. But it's just—it's bad judgment. He should have alerted someone on the night staff who was authorized to do that. Not taken it upon himself."

"How did he get the keys?" Hayden asked.

"He borrowed them from the desk drawer. She gave him a hundred-dollar tip, which is what I guess made him make a bad choice. Anyway, it's very sad. This was Tyler's second summer here and we hate to lose him, but we can't give him another chance." Miss Crossley shook her head. "Everyone, please remember. The rules exist for a reason. To protect you, and to protect the Inn and its guests. Now get back to work."

Claire and I just looked at each other. *Wow,*

she finally mouthed.

"No kidding," I said.

"I thought you were gone for sure," she whispered.

"So did I." I took a sip of orange juice and my hand was shaking from nerves. I'd dodged that bullet. At least . . . I was pretty sure I had. Maybe Mr. Talbot hadn't seen Miss Crossley yet that morning. But he'd have to have been in on the decision to let Tyler go—so he must have kept our secret, as promised. Still, I didn't like the idea he had something to hold over our heads. If we made one more mistake . . . Hayden and I would be gone, too.

Sometimes there are things that you really don't see coming. You think one thing is going to go wrong, and you're completely relieved when it doesn't. So you relax. And then something else hits you.

I'd answered my cell phone while I was back in my room changing clothes for dinner. I figured it was a typical Mom call: Are you doing okay, are you eating right, are you staying out of trouble?

The answers would be yes, yes, and maybe.

But when I answered the phone, she paused for a second after saying hello, which isn't like her at all. She usually begins talking a mile a minute. That made me worry.

"Mom, what's up?" I asked.

"Honey, I'm afraid I have some bad news. Your grandfather—Grandpa McKenzie—"

"What?"

"He's had a heart attack. He's fine, really, but he's in the hospital under the doctors' care and everything's stabilizing now. We don't want you to worry, but we thought you should know—"

"Mom, I'm coming home," I declared.

"Honey, that's not necessary—"

"Yes, it is." I got kind of choked up trying to tell her that. I was about to start crying, but I didn't want to because then she'd worry about me, too, and she had enough to deal with already.

"Well, all right, but what about work?"

"They'll figure it out. Look, I'll get there as fast as I can." I glanced at my watch. It was after six already. "Which hospital, in case I make it in time for visiting hours?"

"County General."

"Mom, I'll have my cell on, so call me—give me an update—tell me stuff, okay?"

"You sure it's okay to leave?"

"It's okay, they'll understand. See you soon." I hung up the phone. Claire wasn't around, so I scribbled a note to her. Then I threw a few changes of clothes into a duffel and ran downstairs and outside to the parking lot.

I threw my bag into the backseat, then slipped the key in the ignition and turned it. Nothing. I tried again. No sound at all. A third time—and it sounded like an old person coughing. And then dying.

Of all the times to have a completely unreliable car. I couldn't stop swearing at it, but that didn't help. I got out and pounded the hood with my fists. Then I grabbed my bag and ran over to the Hullery. It was nearly dinnertime. There had to be someone who could help me, loan me a car—I could beg Miss Crossley if it came to that.

I raced inside and down the steps. I was hoping Claire and Josh would be there, but I didn't see them.

"Can anyone help me?" I said. Then I started to cry, and I hated crying in front of everyone, but I couldn't help myself. "My grandfather — he's had a — a heart attack. I need to get home and see him. My stupid car won't start — does anyone have a car I could borrow? I'm a really good driver, and . . . I'll pay you. Whatever you want."

"I don't have a car here," Richard said.

"Neither do I," Tara added. "I'm sorry, Liza."

Hayden jumped up from his chair. I hadn't even noticed him at the other end of the room. "I don't have a car here, but I can drive you to the train. It's at seven, remember? If we hurry, we can make it."

I vaguely registered the shocked looks on people's faces. I'd been so panicked that I hadn't even remembered there was a train.

"You can get pretty close to home, like New Haven, and get a connecting train, or else your parents or someone could pick you up somewhere along the line. Would that work?" Hayden asked as he came over to me.

"Yeah — that's great. Let's go."

"Wait—I have to ask Miss Crossley, make sure it's okay to take the van," Hayden began. "After this morning—you know."

"You're an authorized driver. We'll call her on the way. I can't miss that train!" I ran up the steps, with Hayden following me.

"Are you and your grandfather close?" Hayden asked as we pulled out of the Inn parking lot. He'd just called Miss Crossley to let her know what was happening, so that was done, which was a relief.

"Kind of. Being an only child—I'm sort of their focus sometimes," I said.

"Is this the grandfather who knows Mr. Talbot Senior?"

I nodded. "Yeah."

"I'll tell him about it when I get back, then. He'd want to know," Hayden said.

"Yeah, I don't know if I would do that. Knowing my grandpa, he'll try to keep this a secret. He wants everyone to still think he's in excellent shape. Which he is, because he runs and swims and hikes. So this heart attack thing, it really doesn't make sense."

Hayden reached over and put his hand over mine. "If he's in great shape, that means he'll recover really quickly."

"Yeah?"

"Yeah. They'll figure out what caused it, maybe give him some medication—"

"What are you, a doctor now?"

"No, but I play one on TV."

I looked over at him and raised one eyebrow. I wasn't in the mood for jokes.

"Okay, so I've watched a lot of TV. And that's what always happens. Totally curable thing," Hayden said.

"Right."

"It's true," he insisted.

I stared out the window for the rest of the trip. I kept picturing my grandfather collapsing, or lying on the ground in pain. Where had he been when it happened? Was my grandmother there? I wondered. She was one of those tough-as-nails people, but even nails had their limits. I couldn't wait to get home and hug her—hug both of them—tightly.

Hayden and I got to the train station with

about ten minutes to spare. I hurried to the ticket window and bought my ticket, then went back to the van for my duffel bag.

"You can take off if you want," I said to Hayden. He was standing beside the van, leaning against it. "The train's on time for once."

"You're kidding. That never happens." He seemed a little disappointed, but maybe he was just stunned. "Well, that's great. You'll get home even faster."

I tried to smile, but I couldn't.

"Don't worry about anything. It's going to be okay. He'll be fine," Hayden said.

I nodded, unable to speak. The reality of what I might have to face at home was sinking in.

"I know you're worried, but your mom said he was okay now. He's in the hospital. They won't let anything happen to him."

I nodded again, and this time felt tears spill down my cheeks. They wouldn't stop coming.

"Liza, don't cry. Please don't cry."

Hayden leaned down and gently pressed his lips against my cheeks, softly kissing the tears. He gathered me in his arms and pulled me close.

I rested my head on his chest, and he put his chin on top of my head.

I didn't move. I couldn't. I didn't want to.

And then I heard the train coming, and I grabbed my duffel and ran.

Chapter Fifteen

My grandfather peered at me through half-awake eyes. My aunt and uncle picked me up at the train station, and I insisted on being taken to the hospital right away. Visiting hours were over by the time we got there, but the nurse said she would let us in anyway, for fifteen minutes.

"If you really want to get out of work, Liza, there are easier ways," my grandfather said.

I rushed to his side and wrapped my arms around his shoulders. "Grandpa, are you okay?"

"I'm perfectly fine," he said. "How are you? And what are you doing here?"

"Mom called—I had to see you. She said you'd be all right, but I wanted to see for myself," I said.

My parents had decided to sit outside in

the waiting room with my aunt and uncle, who'd brought them a late dinner from the outside world.

"They're keeping me here overnight for observation. Isn't that ridiculous? What will they learn by *observing* me?"

"That you're a stubborn old man who hasn't had a checkup in three years," my grandmother said. "That's what."

My grandfather ignored her. "So. How are things at the Inn?"

"Oh, fine," I said with a smile.

"Fine? That's all you're going to tell me about one of my favorite places in the world?"

"Well . . ." I hesitated. "I'm not really here to visit and chat, you know. I'm here to see how *you* are!"

"You've seen. I'm fine. Now tell me a story to take me away from all this." He swept out his arms, knocking a plastic water cup off the tray beside his bed.

My grandparents are the ones I confide in most. They don't tend to overreact the way my parents could. Platinum hair? Jet-black hair? Belly-button piercing? All fine. Or at least not freakworthy. My parents, on the other hand . . . They'd only agreed to let me go away for the summer after my grandparents persuaded them to.

Sometimes I know that what I'm telling my grandparents is going to go straight back to Mom and Dad, but there have been enough times when they *haven't* done that, so I still basically trust them.

Still, was I ready to tell them about Hayden?

"Don't we have more important things to talk about? Like how you are?" I asked my grandfather.

"That's boring. Give us something so we can live vicariously. I'm cooped up in this hospital room when I could be at the beach," Grandpa complained. "What does Bucko have you doing for work? Bill, I mean. Mr. William Talbot Senior, to you."

"Didn't Mom tell you? I'm the official Tides Inn gofer." I explained the various jobs I'd been called on to perform so far.

"Sounds interesting," my grandmother said.

"And what about your social life? Friends?"

"Everyone's been nice," I said.

"And what about Mark?" my grandfather asked.

"Don't pry," Grandma said.

"Too late," Grandpa replied.

"Mark and I? We're on a break."

"What does that mean?" Grandma asked.

"It means . . . I probably have to go talk to him while I'm home. I think I met someone who's . . ."

"Perfect for you?"

Was he? I thought about the way Hayden had held and kissed me that night while we waited for the train. "Yeah, maybe," I said.

"We'll be the judges of that. What's his story?" Grandpa asked.

I laughed. "You're so vague, Grandpa. I never know what you're getting at." I rolled my eyes at him.

"Spill," he said.

Thankfully the nurse came back into the room just then. "It's really time to go," she said to me.

"I'll spill tomorrow," I promised. "Right now

you get back to sleep—I'll come by again in the morning."

I went to find Mark at his uncle's boat factory at 6:45 A.M. As I drove there in my mom's car, I tried not to think about the Inn, but I couldn't help wondering about everyone there and when they'd be getting up and what they'd be doing today. I'd been home for less than twelve hours, but it felt like the longest night in history. I really missed Claire and Hayden and Miss Crossley.

Just kidding on that last one.

I'd tried calling Hayden to tell him everything was okay, but never reached him on his cell. I hadn't spoken to anyone back there yet.

Anyway, I figured catching Mark as he got off his work shift was a good idea. He couldn't avoid me, the way he could if I called ahead. Not that he would, necessarily. But I wasn't sure.

I was sitting on one of the picnic tables outside the factory when he emerged into the early-morning haze. He seemed a little out of it as he rubbed his eyes and focused.

"Yeah, it's me," I said, giving him an awkward little wave.

He said good-bye to his buddies and came over to me.

"Peace offering," I said as I held out a large cup of Dunkin' Donuts coffee to him.

"Thanks. I think."

"I brought doughnuts, too," I said, pointing to the bag on the table. "And a muffin, and a bagel, and—"

"What are you doing here, Liza?" He narrowed his eyes as he slid onto the bench seat across from me. "After all that, don't tell me you quit. Did you quit?"

I shook my head. "No. Not a quitter."

"Right," he said. "SATs. Volleyball. Et cetera."

"Right. So how's your summer been?" I sipped my coffee and reached for the bag to fortify myself with a honey-glazed.

"Are you kidding?" Mark asked.

"No, I'm interested." I tore off a piece of doughnut and put it into my mouth.

"Well. It's been fine. I guess. I work. I hang

out. The usual." He took a blueberry muffin from the bag. Maybe I was here to tell him we were over over, but at least I'd brought his favorite flavor muffin. I wasn't completely horrible. "You?" he asked. "How's the summer?"

"Same as yours. Working, hanging out."

"Is it the dream job you said it was?"

"Yes. And no." Enough beating around the bush; this was getting ridiculous. "Mark? The reason I came home is that my grandfather had a heart attack."

"What? No!" Mark gasped.

"Oh, he's fine. That wasn't the big news."

Mark looked sort of like he wanted to hit me with the blueberry muffin.

"I have something to tell you," I said.

"Yeah, well. Me too," Mark said.

I was thinking his might not be a compliment, so I decided to forge ahead. "I kind of met someone," I blurted. "So—"

"Me too," Mark said, and this sort of sheepish smile crept up the corners of his mouth. Then we both laughed. "Some summer, huh?"

* * *

"Hey, Hayden. Though you told me not to say that. It's Liza. Just wanted to let you know everything's okay. I'll be back tonight—maybe you could pick me up? If you could call me, that'd be great. Okay, bye!"

This was like the tenth time since I'd been home that I'd called and Hayden's phone had gone to voice mail. I hadn't left a message every time—but they were starting to pile up. I could see that if he was already out on the beach, he wouldn't have his phone. But was he going to be working every second of the day?

If so, I'd have to get a message to him another way. As much as I hated to do it, I called the Inn's main number.

"Thank you for calling the Tides Inn, my name is Caroline, how may I assist you?"

"Hey, Caroline. It's Liza," I said.

"Liza who?" she asked.

"Liza McKenzie, who else?" She really killed me with this snobby attitude of hers. "Caroline, where is everyone?"

"What do you mean?"

"Could you tell Miss Crossley I'll be back

tonight? I tried to reach her, but all I got was her voice mail," I explained.

"Oh, well, she's busy organizing the wedding for next weekend. It's Zoe's sister, did you know that?" Caroline asked.

"No. I had no idea," I said.

"It's going to be *so* much fun," she said.

"Great. Look, could you please ask Hayden to pick me up from the train, you know, on the normal shuttle run to the station?" I asked.

"Sure," she said. "I can do that."

"Thanks a lot," I said.

"How's your grandfather?" Caroline asked, seemingly out of the blue. She'd acted like she didn't care, until now.

"Fine, thanks," I said. "He's checking out of the hospital tomorrow, probably."

"Oh, good," she sighed. "He was always so nice to me. Remember how he used to buy us all that saltwater taffy? And the time he and your grandmother took us to Block Island? That was so much fun."

"Yeah, he's great," I said, surprised she remembered and surprised she was being so nice to me for a change. "Hey, thanks a lot,

Caroline. I'll see you soon, okay?"

"Travel safely," she said. "Don't let any weird-oes sit next to you on the train."

I rolled my eyes. "Okay, Caroline."

As much as I'd loved seeing everyone at home, I couldn't wait to get back. I wanted to see the ocean. I wanted to see Hayden.

The train gradually slowed and pulled around the bend, up to the station. I was so anxious to get off of it that I was standing in the door-way with one of the conductors. "You know Hayden?" I asked. "The Tides Inn shuttle driver?"

"I'm sorry?" he said.

"Never mind." I grinned as I saw the van parked in the passenger pickup area. I couldn't wait to tell Hayden that I'd cleared things up with Mark, that we weren't on a temporary summer break anymore—it was permanent. That meant I was really, actually free to date Hayden.

I hopped off the last step onto the platform and walked toward the Tides van. Then I started to run, with a big smile on my face.

And then the driver's side door opened.

And Miss Crossley stepped out.

"Liza, about time you're back. We need you desperately. Hop in."

Funny, that's what I was hoping Hayden would say. *Liza, about time you're back. I need you desperately.*

I tried to hide my disappointment as I stepped up into the van. "I thought maybe Hayden would pick me up," I said. "Isn't he the official shuttle driver?"

"Yes, but he's busy manning the pool tonight because Lindsay had a family emergency, too, and everything's just chaos," Miss Crossley said. She put the van in gear and we pulled away from the station. "Glad everything turned out well at home. Now. About your schedule for the next few days."

I sank down a little in my seat, rolled down my window, and half-listened to her as I breathed in the not-quite-close-enough-to-the-ocean-yet salt air.

Maybe Hayden couldn't leave, like Miss Crossley said, I thought. Maybe it wasn't flat-out rejection.

But that didn't explain why he hadn't called me once while I was gone, or returned any of my calls.

What had I done?

Wasn't our good-bye as romantic as I'd thought it was?

Or had he just been taking pity on me because I was so upset?

Chapter Sixteen

I found Hayden in his room later that night. His roommate, Richard, was there, which made things a little awkward. They were watching a DVD, which they didn't even pause when I walked in.

"Hey, you're back." Hayden glanced over at me. He was lying on his side, on his bed, and he didn't make a move to get up. I was expecting a big hug, not the cold shoulder. What was going on with him?

I went to sit next to him, pushing him over a little to make room. "Yeah, I got back on the train."

"So everything's okay?"

I nodded. "I called you to let you know."

I didn't add "several times," because Richard was sitting there and I was feeling dumb enough already.

"My phone went swimming. Okay, so I went swimming, and it was in my back pocket," Hayden explained. "Anyway, it's history."

"Oh, really?" I said. That seemed like kind of a convenient excuse, but what could I do, disagree with him? I might tease him about it in private, but not in front of his roommate. "So then I asked Caroline to tell you I was coming back, and asked if you could pick me up."

"Oh, yeah? She didn't tell me," Hayden said.

I nodded. "I should have known. She was using her fake voice when I talked to her."

"Which fake voice? She has a few," Richard commented.

"Good point." I smiled at him. Then I looked back at Hayden. "My grandfather's doing really well. It was great to see him and spend some time talking."

"Good," Richard said. "I'm glad he's okay."

Was it me, or was Richard more interested

in what had happened than Hayden? What was going on? "Hey," I said, jiggling his leg. "Are you okay?"

"Oh yeah." He shifted on the bed. "So did you see what's-his-name while you were home?"

Was that hurt in his voice? Jealousy? Or just plain annoyance? "I did see him. But not like you might be thinking. We split up, completely. For good," I said. I spoke softly in case there was any chance of privacy.

"Really." Hayden raised his eyebrows.

"Yes, really." *In fact,* I wanted to say, *I told him I might be seeing someone else. But from the way things look right now, I'd say that I got the wrong impression.*

"Oh yeah? Well, cool. Glad you worked things out." His voice betrayed no emotion at all—not relief, or excitement. Did he really not care at all, or was this just a show in front of his roommate?

"Okay, so . . . you guys enjoy the movie," I said as I got to my feet.

"You want to stick around?" Richard

offered. "I could run down to the Hull, make us some popcorn or something."

I looked at Hayden for my cue. The way things were going a few days ago, I'd have thought: Yes, let's send Richard out on an errand. That'll give us time to be alone. But now? The one who needed to leave was *me*.

"No, that's okay. I have to unpack and things like that. See you, guys," I said as I walked to the door. I turned around as I closed it and made eye contact with Hayden, who was watching me leave. He made no move to get up. He didn't even smile at me.

What did I do? I wanted to scream.

But at the same time, I knew I hadn't done anything. I knew this was all about him.

Upstairs, I stopped in the hallway outside Room 203. The door was open, and inside, Caroline was sitting at her desk, writing in what looked like a journal.

"What are you writing?" I asked.

She slammed the black book closed with a thud. "Nothing."

"Relax, I wasn't going to *read* it." I couldn't

imagine a more boring journal than Caroline's—unless of course she had a secret life. "I have a question to ask you."

"What's that?" She picked up a brush and started to nonchalantly brush her hair.

"Why didn't you give Hayden my message?" I asked.

"Message?" she repeated. She glanced at me in the mirror. "What message?"

"Don't play dumb. I called you from home—we spoke on the phone. I asked you to tell Hayden to come pick me up at the train. Next thing I know, Miss Crossley is there," I said.

"I don't know anything about that," Caroline said.

"You don't." Somehow I found that hard to believe.

"No. Honestly, Liza. I did give him the message. Miss Crossley must have decided she wanted to pick you up herself."

I stared at her for a minute, trying to remember what little tic she had for when she was lying. When we'd gotten into trouble as kids, she was the smooth talker, the one who got us out of things.

"But you know, maybe seeing less of Hayden isn't such a bad idea, if you think about it," she mused.

Did I really want Caroline's opinion on this? But somehow I couldn't resist asking, "Why's that?"

"Because. How well do you know Hayden — really?" she asked.

Better than I know you now, I thought. "Is there something I should know? Besides what you already told me?"

She shook her head. "No, never mind. Look, I'm just — you won't believe me, but I'm trying to look out for you," she said. "I don't think there's anything wrong in being a little cautious when it comes to . . . you know."

"What?" I asked.

She cleared her throat. "Getting . . . involved."

"You mean, being 'really really really close'?" I asked, using her euphemism.

"You know what? Forget it," she said. "Forget I said anything. Do whatever you want.

Just don't come crying to me when it doesn't work out."

"Caroline? Don't worry. For one thing, we're not an item. And for another, if anything did happen? The *last* person I'd come to for sympathy would be you." I walked out of her room without giving her a chance to reply, and into ours next door, slamming both doors behind me.

"Let me guess. You talked to Caroline?" Claire asked, looking up from her book.

"Did I mention I hate dorms?" I said. "There's no privacy anywhere—"

"You want me to leave? I can leave for a while," Claire said. "No problem. If you and Hayden want to talk or whatever—"

"No." I shook my head. "Hayden and I just talked. Or actually I talked, and he just sat there like a lump, as if he didn't even know me or care. I'm done talking to him," I said.

"Let's go out for ice cream." Claire slid her feet into a pair of sandals.

"Really? You think?"

"Let's find Josh and get out of here for a

while." Claire pointed to the wall we shared with Caroline and Zoe.

"Good idea," I said. "I know just where we should go—Sally's."

"Who's Sally?" Claire asked.

"She runs a little coffee place. Come on."

"What are you doing here?" I looked up from the croquet wickets that I was placing in the lawn. "Children are drowning. And don't you have some zinc oxide to apply?"

"Ha. Very funny." Hayden dropped a long duffel that made a clattering wood sound. "I've been replaced."

I couldn't believe it. "What?"

"Yeah. I've been replaced. Go figure," he said. We were standing on the grassy lawn overlooking the ocean, and he pointed at the lifeguard stand, where another figure was perched.

"Like, permanently?" I asked. I could have yelled at myself for having even an ounce of empathy for him. He didn't deserve it. He didn't even deserve me talking to him.

"No, just for this morning," he said. "They

hired someone new, from town, so they can have more of a pool to draw from, in case one of us—or me—gets sick and can't work, or if there's an emergency, like with Lindsay yesterday."

"A pool. Did they actually say that? A pool of lifeguards?" I laughed, despite the fact I felt more like killing him than joking around with him.

"Anyway, that's why I was in such a bad mood last night. Miss Crossley told me about some big event she wants me to help with. The Inn-lympics or something like that?"

"And you brought the mallets?" I asked. "Thanks. So where are all the competitors?"

"Miss Crossley's in the lobby, going over the rules. Quite extensive, from what I gather," Hayden said. "I think she took the actual international Olympics handbook and just modified it a little."

"So. Should we practice?"

Hayden eyed the wickets I'd set up. "Sure."

The air smelled incredible that morning— like flowers and ocean and sunshine. Hayden and I were standing there in our sunglasses and Inn uniforms. We looked like something out of an Inn brochure. This could be such a nice scene.

"What color do you want to be?" Hayden asked.

"Red," I said. The color of anger.

"This is going to be wicket fun," Hayden said in a Boston accent.

It was funny, but I willed myself not to smile. I knocked the ball through the first wicket with one rocket shot.

"Wow. Wicket impressed," he commented.

"I can't believe you," I said as I walked over to it.

"What?" Hayden chose blue and followed behind me. His shot went farther.

"You're such a phony." I whacked the ball again when it was my turn.

"I am? Me?" He knocked through another wicket.

"Yeah. You pretend to be all nice to me, and sweet and romantic, and then when other people are around, it's like you don't even know me. Why?" I asked, sending his croquet ball flying off the grassy lawn and into the sand.

"What are you doing?" he asked. "And what are you talking about?"

We were approaching each other, croquet mallets in hand, and looking vaguely threatening, when Miss Crossley came running out of the Inn. "Liza, stop that!" she cried.

What did she think I was going to do? And why was she only yelling at me, and not both of us? Hayden looked equally murderous.

"We've had an emergency. Roberta's got her hands full because of an especially needy room," Miss Crossley said. "Especially needy" meant "completely trashed" in Tides Inn language. "We need you to help out. Rooms Three-eleven and Three-twelve still need cleaning, and a family's checking into both at noon, they requested early check-in. Could you be a team player and get those two rooms presentable ASAP?"

I'm definitely a team player, but on Uptight Knight's clean team? I wondered. "Are you sure this is okay with Mr. Knight?" I asked.

"Of course. Why wouldn't it be? Anyway, I call the shots around here," she said. "Follow me—Hayden, I'll be right back with the contestants!"

I glared at him as I thrust the red-striped mallet into his arms. "Have a good time."

About an hour later, I was cleaning when there was a knock on the door. I looked up from the coffee table I was dusting, expecting it to be either Roberta or Mr. Knight checking on me. I started dusting more vigorously and sprayed an extra layer of cleaner onto the table. Then I answered, "Yes?"

"Liza? I thought I'd find you here." Hayden stepped into the room.

"Brilliant," I muttered. As if he had figured out something difficult. Miss Crossley had only announced in front of him that I'd be in either Room 311 or 312.

"What's that?" Hayden asked.

"I'm busy," I said.

"This won't take long." He lifted the PRIVACY PLEASE sign off the doorknob and set it on the outside, then he closed the door.

"What are you doing?" I asked. "You can't do that." Of all the times for his infamous daredevil rule-breaking side to come out. "And shouldn't you be competing in the Inn-lympics?"

"I was a referee. A croquet referee. Have you ever heard of anything so lame?" He laughed.

"You can take over in housekeeping anytime," I said under my breath.

"Oh no. I'd never survive. Not neat enough. Let me do my Uptight Knight impersonation." He lifted up the corner of his shirt and ran it over the top of the dresser. "Aha! I have found a speck of dust."

I didn't find him all that amusing. Plus, I couldn't help wondering what he was up to, trapping me in a hotel room. Sure, we lived and worked here, but it was still kind of loaded.

"I can't believe they let you clean again," he said. "After the first time."

"I wasn't that bad," I said. "It was an accident. A runaway vacuum. It could happen to anyone."

He laughed, and I wondered why I was

still trying to be funny, to make him laugh. He didn't deserve it.

"They're checking in soon, so I have to get this done."

"Come on. You can have some fun. So, I was wondering." He switched on the radio beside the bed, then he came over and took the cleaning stuff out of my hands. He ran his finger along my bare arm. "I know this isn't wedding music, but . . . you want to dance?"

I walked over to the radio and snapped it off. "You know, I was wondering something, too. What is your problem?"

"My problem?" he asked.

"With acknowledging me. With being in public together," I said.

He paced around the room for a second, walking over to the window and back again. "It's not you, it's me," he finally said.

I laughed. "What soap opera did you hear that on?" I scoffed. "And anyway—no kidding. It is you. We could be together. We could be *great* together, if you haven't noticed. But you've got some weird hang-up where you only want to think that some of the time," I said.

He finally sighed and sat down at the desk. "Okay, fine. You want an explanation. You know what it is? I hated how last year everyone knew about me and Zoe. I hated it. They all had their opinions, like they felt like they could discuss us. I didn't want that to happen again."

"Didn't want *what* to happen again?" I asked. "The girlfriend part or the gossip part?"

He swiveled back and forth in the chair. "The everyone-in-my-business part."

"I don't think that's it," I said. "I think you're, like, embarrassed of me, for some reason. I think you just don't want everyone to know about *me*."

Hayden shook his head. "That's not it. I just like to keep things private."

"Keep me private, you mean."

"Keep what happens between us private," he said. "That's why I put the sign on the door. Privacy please. Like if I could wear one of those around my neck."

"That could be arranged," I said. Very, very tightly.

"What do you want me to do?"

I was so angry, I couldn't even talk to him.

"I don't know," I said. "But not what you've been doing."

"Look, if you want to find me, I'll be back at the beach later, from one to four," he said, and then he stood up and left the room.

Great. Now I couldn't even go to the beach.

Chapter Seventeen

So I'd go to another beach, I decided once Miss Crossley released me for the day—or "for the time being," as she liked to say.

No problem.

I'd go to one in Newport. Or I'd catch the ferry to Block Island. Would that be far enough away?

Sure. But to get all those places, I had to drive and my car still wouldn't start. I was sitting in the scorching hot driver's seat, turning the ignition again and again, but nothing was happening.

Why did I have a feeling I'd be leaving my car at the Inn at the end of the summer, along with my hopes of a big romance? Not that Miss Crossley would let me abandon my car. She'd have it towed to the nearest junkyard. In fact, I was surprised she hadn't already done that—maybe she hadn't noticed it yet.

All of a sudden the passenger door opened, and Hayden stuck his head inside the car. "I didn't realize this loud screeching sound was your car. I thought it was a flock of seagulls that'd just spied a bag of potato chips."

I laughed, despite the fact I'd wanted to kill him the last time I saw him. "It does sound like that, doesn't it?"

"Let me try something," Hayden said.

"Hurry up, I think my legs are melting onto the seat," I said.

He closed the door, then pounded the hood a few times with the heel of his hand. "That didn't work, did it? So come on, go for a bike ride with me."

"It's going to start this time," I said as I turned the key in the ignition.

"No, it isn't. Your belts are shot, or one of them is, anyway." He peered in at me through my open window. He looked really good today, in a faded brown T-shirt and baggy green army shorts. "You're a belt killer. You know that?

That's like twelve this summer."

"It's not *twelve*," I said as I got out of the car, the seat making a sticky sound. "Three or four, tops."

"That's not the point. The point is that biking to the beach is a lot more fun."

Fun with Hayden. Had I completely given up on that yet? "What kind of bike are we talking about?" I asked, narrowing my eyes.

"It's a mountain bike. Practically brand-new and totally nice," Hayden said. "I checked out all the bikes in the shed and it's probably the best one in there."

I was so tempted. It was about four thirty, and I really wanted to spend the rest of the day— and evening—away from the Inn. But the thing was, part of the reason I felt that way was because I needed to get away from Hayden. So how would spending my night off with him help?

"But I'm still mad at you," I told Hayden. "So I probably shouldn't."

"So ride behind me and spend the first hour yelling at me," Hayden said.

"You're going to wear headphones, aren't

you?" I accused him.

"I'm considering it. How mad are you?" he asked.

"How far are we going?"

"I don't know. It's up to you. I was thinking we could ride somewhere, grab some takeout, maybe hit a different beach or something." He shrugged. "Whatever."

It totally went against common sense, kind of like getting a belly button pierced, as Miss Crossley saw it. I'd tried so hard to stand my ground with Hayden, to tell him what he was doing wrong. And part of me knew I shouldn't go anywhere with him until we had another "talk." But that wasn't the fun, adventurous part of me. Which was screaming, *What are you waiting for?*

"Whatever sounds great," I said. "Just let me grab my backpack."

"This is sort of creepy."

"I know, isn't it?" Hayden asked.

We were standing outside a large hotel about five miles up the coast from the Tides

Inn. But instead of looking exclusive, it looked excluded—from guests, from renovations, from everything. The white paint was peeling, a few windows were broken, and the main entrance had a door that sagged.

"It's like a lesson, what could happen if the Tides ever closed," I said.

"If it ever closed, people would buy up the land in a second. I can't remember why the owners of this won't sell yet, but they refuse."

Hayden opened the door and we walked inside the old inn. "It only closed two summers ago. Mismanagement of funds or something like that," he explained. "Wouldn't it be amazing to buy this place?"

"And compete with the Tides? Peach would never forgive you," I told him.

"No, I suppose not. But wouldn't that be okay?" Hayden smiled. "No, actually I like Miss C. I mean, there's something cool about being that reliable, that consistent, all the time."

"Sure there is," I said. "I just haven't figured out what yet."

I heard a creaking sound and felt a shiver

crawl up my spine. I'm not one to jump at the slightest noise or scare easily—usually. But something about this place was giving me the creeps.

"Don't worry about that sound. It only means the ghosts are out walking today," Hayden said.

"What ghosts?" I asked.

"Former guests. There was a double murder here back in the seventies," Hayden said. "People say that's what brought bad luck to the place."

I laughed nervously. "Maybe C. Q. Wallace should come here if he's still looking for material." I stepped closer to Hayden. "Do you think maybe we could go back outside?"

"Are you wimping out on me? That's not like you. Come on, let's check out the upstairs," Hayden urged.

"Did you ever read the book or see that movie *The Shining*, about that creepy deserted hotel in Colorado?" I asked. "Because this is reminding me of that."

"You're not the type of person to let this scare you. Are you? I mean, are you afraid of ghosts?" Hayden asked.

"No. Not really. But what if there are live people up here?" I asked as we ascended the creaky staircase.

"There won't be. The police come through here all the time," Hayden said with confidence.

I put my hand on his arm, trying to stop him. "Which is another reason we should go."

We both paused at the top of the stairs, and gazed into a room's open doorway. "Whoa," I exhaled. "If Uptight Knight saw this, he'd go berserk."

"More berserk," Hayden said.

"Berserkier," I added.

The room was stripped bare of furniture except for an old, rusted metal blanket rack, and a dust-covered desk that was missing a leg and listed to one side. A coffeemaker with mold growing inside sat on a desk, and the carpet smelled of something rotten.

"Okay, I think I need to take a shower just from looking at this place," I said.

"Yeah, me too. I haven't been here since last summer when a whole bunch of us came over," Hayden said. "It's a lot more, uh . . ."

"Disgusting?" I suggested.

"How about a swim to get the dirt off?" Hayden brushed at his arms. "This hotel has a private beach just like the Tides, and at least that can't have gotten trashed."

"Let's go!" I said. We ran down the stairs, out the front door, and down the path to a small sandy beach.

"Where do we change?" I asked.

"Over there." Hayden pointed to a small beach hut connected to the hotel that looked like it could have been a cabana, once upon a time.

"No thanks," I said. "Not if it's anything like the inside of *that* place."

"Good point. Here, you change behind that dune." Hayden pointed to a grassy area that dipped down below the level of the rest of the property. I could probably conceal myself there, but still . . .

"I don't know. What if someone shows up?" I asked.

"Who's going to come here?"

"If you know about it, don't other people? And what if the police come by?" I asked.

"I'll stall them until you're decent," Hayden offered. He picked up my backpack from the sand and tossed it to me. "Unless you'd rather swim in your clothes? Or without them?"

"Fat chance. I'll be back in a minute," I told him.

We raced each other to be first into the ocean. It was becoming a tradition with us—except this time, for once, I won.

I wasn't sure if that was a good thing as I came up gasping for air. I'd definitely chosen a cold spot to dive into.

"Did they lose their lease on decent temperature water, too?" I asked.

"The current must be slightly different here," Hayden said.

"You know, I always knew the Inn was exclusive, but I mean, are they *that* sheltered, from even the elements of nature?" We started to swim in the deeper water.

"You kind of have an attitude about the Inn and its guests. Do you think they're all spoiled?"

"Aren't they? I don't know. Maybe I'm just

not cut out for customer service," I said.

We swam side by side for a few minutes, and I noticed Hayden kept glancing at the shore.

"Why do you keep looking at the hotel? Is someone there?" I stopped swimming and treaded water.

"No, don't worry so much. It's important to keep aligned with something onshore, so you don't mistakenly go too far out. If you ever get caught in a riptide, you've got to swim parallel to the beach until you get out of it."

"I've heard that," I said. "I think it happened to my grandmother once, and she swam out of it. But . . . are we *in* a riptide?"

"No. More like high tide." Hayden laughed.

"I have to say, it's pretty cool having my own personal lifeguard," I said as we swam back toward shore. I reached for the ocean bottom with my feet, finally touching sand. Hayden and I stood halfway in and halfway out of the water.

"Hold on, you're coming untied," he said.

Unglued was more like it. He was standing so close to me, his hands on my shoulder as he retied the stringy strap around my neck. I held my breath. The anticipation was killing me.

"How many swimsuits do you have, exactly?" Hayden asked. "I've counted three, so far."

"Four," I said.

"Oh. So I have something else to look forward to." He ran his fingers from my suit strap down my back.

"You could say that." I put my hands on his strong, tanned shoulders and felt the muscles of his upper arms.

Were we really doing this? I was so caught up in the moment that I barely had time to think. And yet I knew that I'd already decided I was ready to take this step with Hayden. But maybe I was assuming too much—maybe he wasn't ready.

"Do you think there is a PRIVACY PLEASE sign we could put on the beach?" Hayden asked.

"Why?" I asked. "Is anyone around that we need to worry about?"

"Just us. And maybe this will sound totally crazy, but that's what I want. Because . . . this is going to sound dumb, okay? But I feel like I can't get enough of you."

"It's not dumb. That's how I feel about you," I confessed.

We started to kiss, and then we started to shiver because the sun was setting, and a cold breeze was coming off the water.

"We should probably go," Hayden said.

I knew he was right, but I hated to admit that. "Probably," I said.

We walked out of the water, holding hands. "The sand's still warm, though," Hayden observed.

I glanced at him and smiled. I wasn't sure I should really do this. I should either leave now or be prepared for the consequences. Was I ready for this?

Yes.

"I have a beach blanket." I crouched by my backpack and pulled it out. I unfolded the blanket and shook it out, placing it on the beach. As soon as I sat down, Hayden lay down beside me. I lay back on the blanket, too.

We looked at each other for a few seconds,

as if we were both making sure we knew how serious this was getting.

Hayden propped himself up on his elbow. He pushed a strand of my wet hair behind my ear. "I had a really good time with you today."

I reached up and touched him gently on the lips. "Me, too."

He kissed my fingers and then didn't move for a second. He just kept looking into my eyes. "Liza?" he finally said.

I was starting to feel nervous about what he might say. *Please don't say we should take off. I don't want to leave now.* "Hayden?" I replied, a little breathless.

"I think . . . I think maybe I'm falling in love with you," he said.

"Really?"

"Really."

"Good," I said.

He laughed. "Why is that good? It's sort of torture if you ask me—"

"Because I'm falling in love with you, too," I admitted.

"Then we're even," he said.

"Even? What is this—a competition—" I started to say, but Hayden silenced me with a kiss.

To my right, in my backpack, I could hear a beeping sound. My pager was stuffed in the outside pocket.

I started to get up to check it, but then I stopped.

It wasn't about Grandpa, because they'd call my cell. So it was definitely work.

This time, Miss Crossley would have to wait.

I wasn't about to leave where I was right now.

Chapter Eighteen

"That's the second time you haven't responded to a page."

Miss Crossley had paged me to her office first thing the next morning, to yell at me for not responding to her pages.

"The first time, I was in Newport and it was my day off," I said in self-defense. "And this time . . . well . . ." Did she really want to know what I was up to with Hayden? I definitely didn't want to tell her. Besides, I'd barely gotten used to admitting it to myself. "I didn't hear it," I said. "Honestly. It did not make a sound."

At least, not a sound that I wanted to hear. What is the sound of one pager buzzing? If a pager buzzes in a backpack and no one hears it . . . did it really buzz?

My stomach made a loud grumbling noise, and I realized I needed to grab some breakfast soon—very soon. Hayden and I had never gotten around to picking up that takeout meal, and by the time we got back to the Inn, the Hull was shut down for the night. We'd snuck into the dorm, it was so late.

"Well, if you say so. Perhaps you were out of range." She gave me a suspicious look.

I wasn't about to volunteer any information about how I'd spent the evening. "Out of range" wasn't a bad description, though. I thought about what Hayden had said: *I think I'm falling in love with you.*

"All right. Let's move on." Miss Crossley stacked a set of papers on her desk. "Today's assignment."

I loved the way she made it sound as if I were a secret agent. Secret agents didn't do dishes or clean toilets, though. At least, not the cool ones.

"C. Q. Wallace. You've become acquaintances, yes?" Miss Crossley asked.

I shrugged. "You could say that."

"You have a certain rapport. And he needs someone to help him with his manuscript," Miss Crossley said. "We've selected you because he already knows you, for one, and because it says in your application that you're a good typist."

I loved the thought of this assignment, but the beach was calling me. I wanted to be on the beach, with Hayden, not cooped up inside doing office work. I didn't care how many sand castles I had to help build, how many games of Wiffle ball I had to play. They could give me twenty kids to look after, just as long as I got to be near Hayden.

"But Miss Crossley. Is it really the Inn's place to help him with his book?" I asked.

Miss Crossley looked completely stunned, as if I had suggested stoning the author with rocks from the beach. "Yes, Liza, it's our place to help him, if it means he'll stay here longer. Do you know what long-term guests mean to this place? Survival, Liza."

I thought of the closed and shuttered hotel Hayden and I had visited the day before, which reminded me of why I hadn't answered her page. I felt a blush creep up my entire body, from my toes to my torso to my face to my scalp under my Tides Inn ball cap (where thankfully, it was concealed).

No matter what Miss Crossley said? Even if she docked my paycheck? I wouldn't regret ignoring that pager. I was still kind of in shock about it, though.

"So what would this involve?" I asked.

"I believe he has a handwritten rough draft he needs to have typed. Something about carpal tunnel. You'll work side by side for today, and possibly more days in the future."

"So . . . no outdoor time? At all?" I asked. I felt like a dog stuck in a kennel.

"We'll see how it goes. You'd better go see him — he'll meet you in the lobby at ten," Miss Crossley said. "Oh, and Liza?" she asked as I stood up to leave. "That's the second time I've tried to page you and you haven't been around. Let's not have a third, all right?"

She didn't come right out and say that it was my last chance — that if I got a third strike, I'd be out — but I could tell that was what she meant. It wasn't fair, because I was the only employee who was on call all the time. But I sensed now wasn't the time to point that out to her. If she wanted me to be there for her — I'd be there.

"What's the book about?" I asked as I turned on the notebook computer C. Q. had brought downstairs to the back porch. He'd already plugged it into an outlet, so there was no hope of the battery running out and my job finishing early.

"It's about identity, love, American history, and . . . oh, you'll find out soon enough. It's a novel about a family that vacations at a large Rhode Island hotel."

"Kind of like *The Shining*?" I asked.

He frowned at me. "No. Great book, but no. This isn't a horror novel."

"So this large inn — is it based on this place?" I said.

"No. Resemblance to anything or anyone is strictly coincidental. Or whatever they print at the beginning of the book that means I can't be sued." He coughed and put out his cigarette.

"Anyhow, it's not this place. It's a composite, of many hotels I've stayed at."

"In Rhode Island," I said. "Uh huh. Fine, whatever you say. Except you should probably change my *name*," I insisted as I typed in an exchange between the main character and an employee of the hotel. "And why did you make me short? I don't want to be short."

"It's fiction. Let it go," he advised.

"And speaking of names," I went on. If he could use mine, then I had a question about his. "What does C. Q. stand for?"

"Don't tell anyone. But nothing. I just liked the initials. My real name is Larry."

"Larry?" I wanted to giggle, but resisted.

"I know, Larry Wallace doesn't have quite the same cachet as a pair of pretentious initials."

"You're right. Larry Wallace sounds like someone who works at the car repair shop, or a phys ed teacher or something."

"My point exactly. What were my parents thinking?" He laughed. "They scarred me for life."

Caroline came out onto the back porch. She

was watching us, but pretending *not* to watch us. "Checking the surf again?" I asked her.

"What?" she said in an innocent tone.

"Nothing." I kept typing.

"Wow. Liza, I didn't know you were a secretary," Caroline said.

"She's my creative assistant today," C. Q. said. "Now, could you get us some coffee?"

"I'm sorry?" Caroline looked highly offended.

"Don't be sorry. Just get us the coffee," C. Q. said.

I bit my lip to keep from smiling.

"I'll try to—to—find your, uh, server," she said.

"Or you could do it," C. Q. said.

"I can go do it," I offered, standing up. "If I'm your assistant, then—"

"No, you're not going for coffee, you're going for a land-speed record, typing this manuscript for me. Carry on. I take mine black," he said to Caroline. She made a tsking noise and walked away.

"*You* need to stay right here. The fewer

distractions, the better." He stared at the beach for a second. "Oh, great. Here comes distraction number one."

What was he talking about? I looked up and saw Hayden walking toward the Inn. He must be on break. Just seeing him, I felt this magnetic pull.

"Keep your mind on your work."

"Sir, yes sir," I replied. "But anyway. Why do you say that?"

"I saw you two. I've seen you two."

"What?"

"Never mind," he said.

I glanced over at C. Q. (Larry), a new cigarette dangling from his lip, writing in a notebook. While I typed, maybe he could use up some more pens, I thought, or notebooks. Then Hayden and I would have the perfect excuse to escape together.

Maybe he could run out of his famous Turkish cigarettes. And maybe Hayden and I would have to go to Turkey—or at the very least Providence—to buy some more. If Miss Crossley wanted me to keep a long-term guest happy, I was willing to do my part. As long as Hayden went with me.

I had to work so late that night that by the time I got back to the dorm, it was nearly eleven. I'd missed the party at Crandall's Point—sitting on the porch and then after dark in the lobby typing, I'd heard everyone go rushing by. I'd missed everything. My back was killing me. But Mr. Wallace had his pages ready to send off, so tomorrow I'd have a break. I was more than ready to try something else.

I couldn't wait to see Hayden—being away from him for the entire day had been pure torture. Even though it was late, I decided to stop by his room to say hi before I turned in for the night.

I was about to knock on the door when I heard Hayden's voice. "I don't want to hurt her, but I have to tell her before tomorrow," he was saying.

Was he talking about me?

"So tell her," Richard said.

"I can't. She likes me now. She won't like me

after I tell her," Hayden said.

I stepped back from the door. I was feeling really scared. I'd totally fallen for him. I'd slept with him. What did he have to tell me that was so horrible?

I definitely didn't feel like barging in right that second and finding out. Not without checking in with Claire first. I'd go upstairs — maybe he'd left me a note, saying he needed to talk. When he was ready, he'd come find me — probably he'd been waiting all night for me to show up.

I went up to our room. There was no note and no Claire. Where could she be this late? I kicked off my sandals and sat on the edge of my bed, letting out a big, tense sigh. What was Hayden talking about? I took a deep breath and tried to collect myself.

You've got to go back downstairs right now, I told myself. You have to find out what this is about.

And I would — in just a few more minutes. I lay back on the bed, completely exhausted by the last forty-eight hours.

* * *

I never went back down to talk to Hayden. I fell asleep and slept so hard that the next day I slept right through breakfast, then got woken up by Miss Crossley pounding on the door, telling me to meet her at the Inn's main doors, at the shuttle pickup. I had vague hopes of seeing Hayden, but instead it was an Inn kids' trip to play miniature golf, race in go-karts, and hit in batting cages.

(They tried to do all that stuff without me, but I wouldn't let them. No way was I spending the entire day *observing*.)

Miss Crossley dropped us off at the amusement park at ten and came back for us at four. By the time she fetched us, almost all of us had sunburns and were completely exhausted from the intense heat and activity.

I had just enough time to rush to the dorm, shower, heavily apply aloe lotion, throw on my catering clothes, run back to the kitchen, and take my tray of champagne and sparkling water out to the dining room.

When I walked in, I looked around for the

bride, knowing it was Zoe's sister, Anneke. I wanted to see how much she and Zoe looked alike. I couldn't find Anneke at first, because she and the groom were mingling, but I did spot them across the dining room.

I spotted Zoe next.

And then I saw Hayden.

There, sitting at the head table beside Zoe, was Hayden, wearing a dark-blue suit and looking extremely handsome.

What was he doing there? He didn't tell me he was going to the wedding.

They're old family friends, I tried to tell myself. They go way back.

Don't they?

Okay, so they were from the same town, so why wouldn't he be at her sister's wedding? It made sense. It was all extremely innocent and platonic.

Then I saw the wedding photographer stop at the table to take a photo, just as I was walking in that direction to say hi to both of them.

"Come on, everyone, say cheese. Kiss for the camera!" the photographer urged, and somebody in the crowd started to ring their glass with a knife, so the married couple would kiss.

Hayden put his arms around Zoe's shoulder, and then he pressed his lips against Zoe's cheek. She turned her head and he kissed her right on the mouth.

Chapter Nineteen

*T*he champagne glasses tumbled off my tray and onto the floor.

Fortunately I was in the carpeted area at the time, so instead of shattering and drawing everyone's attention to me, they just sort of bounced and knocked into each other, splashing my shoes with champagne.

Unfortunately I let out a little shriek as it happened. So everyone looked at me anyway.

I caught Hayden looking over at me with a startled expression, and I glared right back at him. If I didn't strangle him now, it was only because there were about two hundred witnesses.

Was that why everything between us always

had to be a secret, because he was still trying to get back together with Zoe? Or had he been with her this whole time—while he was also with me?

Was I the stupidest girl on the planet— or in Rhode Island—or what? *Everyone knew,* I thought. *Everyone knew except me.*

Caroline knew—she tried to warn me to stay away from Hayden, in her own weird way. Richard knew—that was why he was so nice to me, because he pitied me. Maybe even Claire knew, and that was why she kept warning me against dating Hayden. Everyone else who'd ever hung out at Crandall's Point probably knew Hayden and Zoe still had a "thing." Or something. And they were all looking at me.

She likes me now, Hayden had said last night to his roommate. *She won't like me after I tell her.*

He was right. I wouldn't like him anymore, now that I knew he wanted to see two girls at the same time.

Uptight Knight was on me immediately. "Do you know how impossible it is to get the smell of alcohol out of carpet?"

I turned to him and raised my eyebrow. "We'll Febreze it."

Claire and Josh found me in the kitchen, where I was collecting myself by drinking iced tea mixed with lemonade and snacking on shrimp cocktail.

I must have downed five or six consecutive shrimp without really pausing, because the plate—which was supposed to go onto the tray and be served—was now empty.

"Where have you been?" Josh asked. "One whole table didn't get their champagne and we had to scramble for more glasses just in time for the big toast."

"Where have I *been*? Didn't you see me?" I asked.

They both shook their heads.

"You didn't see what happened? Well, that's two people out of two hundred. You must not have been in the dining room when it happened. I had a little accident. Dropped my tray. Screeched when I did it. Fortunately it was on carpet, but I got splashed."

"So you're in here recovering from spillage?" Claire asked.

"You could say that." I brushed a speck of lint off my black skirt, part of my official catering gear uniform. "You could also say that I'm recovering from seeing Hayden with Zoe. I mean, what *is* that?"

I wandered over to the kitchen doorway and looked out at the scene. Yup, Hayden and Zoe were still sitting next to each other. They didn't seem to be talking, at the moment, but that was because they were both eating.

"I noticed they were at the same table," Josh said.

"I guess their families are pals—you said they came from the same town, right?" Claire asked. "So he must have gone to the wedding—you know, as a friend."

"That's what I tried to tell myself. But would a *friend* sit at the head table with the bride and groom and wedding party?" I asked.

"It's a pretty big table. So maybe," Claire said.

I glared at her. "Hey, I'm the optimist, not

you. And would he kiss her on the mouth? Tell me—is it as bad as it looks?"

"It's not *good*," Claire said.

"I have an idea. Josh, dance with me," I said.

He groaned. "Please don't make me do that."

"One dance. It won't kill you."

"You don't know that. Have you heard the music?" Josh pretended to stick his finger down his throat.

I laughed. "Okay, so the music's kind of cheesy, but come on, just a quickie."

"Well, if *that's* what we're talking about—"

"We're not." I grabbed the sleeve of Josh's white button-down shirt and pulled him out of the kitchen, toward the dance floor, with Claire following close behind us.

"You'll owe me for this," Josh said as I put my hands on his shoulders, and he rested his hands on my waist.

"I know. I already do," I said.

We moved around the dance floor, staying in the middle so that Miss Crossley wouldn't notice us. I tried to dance close enough to

Hayden's table that he'd see us. Two could play that game. He wanted to have someone on the side? So did I.

Okay, not really, but I might be able to make it look that way.

"Take it easy," Josh said, as I leaned my cheek against his shoulder.

"Too close?" I asked.

"A little," he said.

I know Hayden saw us, because he and I exchanged yet another awkward glance.

Cut in anytime, I thought. *Cut in and show me—and everyone else—that we're together now, the way you said we were the other night.*

But he didn't budge. He sat there beside Zoe, taking part in the conversation at the table, without moving. I turned away; that was something I didn't need to see over and over.

The song came to an end, and I felt a tap on my shoulder.

I turned around, my heart beating faster.

"Excuse me, but aren't you employees?" a man in a black tuxedo asked. "Are you supposed to be dancing? I mean, this is my daughter's wedding, and if you're dancing, then what are we paying you for?"

I don't know, I thought, *but nobody's paying me nearly enough to put up with this.*

"Don't you have cake to hand out?" Zoe's father asked.

"Sorry, sir. We got caught up in the moment," I said. *The moment where I want to throttle your other daughter and her apparent date.* "It won't happen again."

"Got that right," Josh muttered as we headed off the dance floor.

I passed right by Miss Crossley, who was walking through the lobby in the opposite direction. "I'll be back, I promise," I told her, hoping that Zoe's dad wouldn't complain to her about me and Josh dancing. "I just need some fresh air."

"But—Liza—this is highly irregular—"

No kidding, I thought. "Ten minutes, okay? I really have to do this," I said.

She gave me a stunned look as I bolted out the back door. I ran past guests on the porch and nearly knocked down a woman walking back up from the beach.

Then I heard heels clattering on the board-walk behind me. "Liza! Liza, wait up!" a female voice called.

I turned around and saw Caroline coming. She ran toward me, tossing her stilettos onto the sand, her fancy strapless dress (because she was a wedding guest, too) rippling in the wind. "Are you okay?"

I couldn't believe her nerve. "No. Not really," I said. "But you told me not to come crying to you. So I won't."

"I'm sorry," Caroline said. "I shouldn't have—"

"You know what, Caroline? You could have just told me. You had every opportunity in the world."

"Yeah, I guess I could—but I wasn't—I didn't really think they'd go through with it. They both wanted to call it off, but—"

"But what?"

"It was all arranged. A long time ago."

"So I was merely messing up their social calendar? You know what? Forget it. I don't want to know." I didn't want to listen to her, of all people, *explain* this to me.

I took off jogging down the beach, kicking the surf with my feet, wishing I'd come anywhere except the Inn for the summer.

Chapter Twenty

*H*ayden was sitting in the hallway outside my door when I got back to the dorm, around two in the morning. His suit was rumpled, his tie untied.

I really, really wanted to talk to him. And I also really didn't ever want to see him again.

Was he waiting for me? Or was he just slumped there because he'd been in Zoe's room, which happened to be right next door to mine?

This dorm stuff sucked. It was like living in a fish bowl. And I was starting to feel like that one pathetic fish that's always at the edge of the bowl, staring straight ahead like it can't wait to escape.

If dorm life was what college was all about,

then maybe I should reconsider going away to college and stay home.

"Where have you been all night?" Hayden asked.

I was holding my sandals, and my legs and ankles were covered in sand that looked like a dusting of cinnamon and sugar. I'd tried to wash it off before I came inside, with the hose by the door, but sort of halfheartedly. If sand got all over the dorm, what did I care?

"I was walking on the beach," I told him. "Then I lay down to look at the stars and I guess I fell asleep."

"You slept on the beach," Hayden said.

"Yup."

"By yourself."

What was he implying? Did he really think I'd be out there with someone else? "Yup."

Hayden scrambled to his feet. "Do you know how dangerous that is?" He gave me this pleading look. "Promise me you won't do that again."

"It's not dangerous. I sleep with one eye open."

"Right," Hayden said.

"How long have you been waiting?" I asked.

"Or did you just pass out here after the big wedding night?"

"I've been here since midnight," Hayden said. "Since Zoe and everyone else at the wedding crashed at the Inn. They rented the second and third floors, you know?"

"Fascinating." I opened the door to our room and walked inside.

I couldn't believe it. Claire wasn't home. Claire, who I'd been counting on to get me out of this. She was not in her bed.

Hayden, apparently seeing that she wasn't there, followed me into my room and closed the door behind him.

I walked over and opened it a crack. It wasn't that I was scared of him, or what would happen. I just didn't want him to think that he could have me all to himself. I was too mad to want to be alone with him. Let Caroline hear us argue, too. Maybe she could tell Zoe what happened.

"I didn't know how to tell you," Hayden began.

Oh God. Anything but that. What a horrible thing to say.

"My family was coming and I was all stressed out about that and I didn't know what to say."

"So you didn't tell me anything."

"Don't hate me," Hayden said. "I had to do it."

"Had to do what?"

"Had to be at the wedding today. It's—it's complicated."

"Not really," I said. "You and Zoe still being together is actually not all that complex."

"But we're *not* still together, you know that."

"Do I?" I asked.

"Yes."

"I thought I did, until today. Then everything started to look a lot different."

"You don't understand." Hayden paced back and forth between our beds, which was a pretty small space to use for pacing. "Our families— they expect us—they want us to be together."

"What?" I laughed. "Are you serious? This is the twenty-first century. Are you trying to tell me you guys have an arranged marriage or something like that? Because this isn't exactly the culture where that is the norm. So I don't think that's it. What's the problem, then? Am I not good enough for you? Because that's ridiculous."

"Of course you're good enough for me," Hayden said. "But our parents—they have these ideas. So I agreed to go to the wedding with Zoe, to make her parents happy, which makes my parents happy."

"I don't understand. But I do know that I can't—I don't—trust either of you. If you can't stand up to your parents—I mean, you're in college—and you're still letting them tell you what to do?"

"I don't have a choice. They expect things from me."

"And they don't expect . . . what? You to be with a completely scandalous girl from *Connecticut*? Ooh, scary. Do they restrict other states? What about Rhode Island, is that out?" I snapped my fingers. "I know. It's because I don't go to stupid Maple Syrup Acad—"

"I'm sorry, but I don't want to rock the boat

right now. Too much is happening," Hayden said. "I was all worried about my mom and dad and whether they'd fight, and it took them like two seconds before they got into an argument, and then my sister, Grace, gets out of the car and she's wearing black lipstick and combat boots to a wedding—"

I started to feel sympathy for him, remembering our conversation on the beach about his family. But what was he saying? They'd been at the wedding—and he hadn't introduced me? All my sympathy was gone as I realized that. I'd never treat him like that!

"I want to be with you, Liza. You know that."

"I thought I did. But does anyone else? I mean in some ways, you're acting just like Caroline."

"What?"

"You're being a total snob! Whenever I try to bring up stuff we used to do together, she pretends it didn't happen, that it wasn't me she hung out with. And you do the same thing," I said. "Your parents aren't the only ones you're hiding from. You never want to be around me when *any* other people are there. It's like we have no history. You always find some reason to take off—"

"I do not. I don't know what you're talking about," Hayden said. "Everyone knows about us."

"If they do, it's not because of you!" I started to say, just as the door popped open. Claire backed into the room, Josh kissing her.

"Ex—excuse us," Josh said.

"Oh. Oh my God. I thought you guys would be, uh, out," Claire said. "Kissing and making up. Not in that order."

"We didn't exactly make up," I said.

"And we're not going to tonight," Hayden added.

"No. We're not," I said.

"Fine!" Hayden went out and slammed the door behind him.

"What's he so mad about? You're the one who should be mad," Josh said.

"Oh, I am," I said. "I'm furious." Then I sank onto my uncomfortable, flat bed and curled up into a fetal position. "I just *really* like him," I confessed.

"Like . . . in love?" Josh asked.

"I don't know. I guess I am, sort of. And I thought it would be fun, but it isn't and I hate it."

Josh gave me a sympathetic smile, as if I had an illness that couldn't be cured. "Well, I'll let you guys talk. 'Night." He leaned over to rub my head, then he quickly kissed Claire before leaving.

"Claire?" I said the second the door closed. "All those things you told me about not—"

"I know, I know. But I couldn't help it," she said. "He's so cute and funny. I just want to be with him all the time—"

"Well, that's how I feel. No, that's how I felt," I corrected. Until tonight.

"Which is it?" Claire asked.

"Feel. Present tense. But with a lot of emphasis on *tense*. So when did you and Josh get together?"

"I actually have you to thank for that," Claire said. "When you asked him to dance this afternoon? I wanted to kill you. That's when I realized he couldn't dance with anyone but me. I mean, we'd gone out once, but you know me. I usually have my one-date limit."

"You were out so late tonight, I think that counts as three dates."

"But what about you and Hayden? What are you going to do?" Claire asked.

I shrugged. "I have no idea."

"You know what? In spite of everything, I don't think he's a bad person. I really don't. I think he's confused, you know? And he made some bad choices."

"You're only saying that 'cause you're in love."

"I'm not in love," Claire said. "I'm in like. I'm having fun, for once."

"Okay, but you'll be spending so much time with Josh this summer, you'll probably never make it through all those serious books now," I teased her. "You realize that."

"Oh, well. Columbia will understand why I ditched the reading list," she said. "Right?"

Chapter Twenty-one

"*B*ut Miss Crossley—"

"You love the beach," she said.

I nodded. "I know. I do. I really do."

I wanted to say: And any other day, even tomorrow, it might be okay. But not this morning. Please, not this morning.

"I was just hoping . . . I really got into typing that book the other day. I kind of can't wait to see how it turns out. I was thinking maybe I could work with Mr. Wallace again."

Miss Crossley dusted her telephone while she talked. "That would be extremely difficult, seeing as how he checked out yesterday morning."

"No, he didn't," I said. "He couldn't have."

"What? Do you know something I don't?"

"He—he can't check out! He didn't even tell me he was leaving!" I protested.

Miss Crossley shifted in her office chair, looking a little uncomfortable. "Oh no. Do you and Mr. Wallace have some kind of personal, ah, relationship—"

"No, of course not. Nothing like that." I shook my head. "We were friends, that's all." And I had been hoping to lean on him today, like a crutch, I thought. He could tell me how love sucked, how high the divorce rate was, and what a load of garbage romance was, and I'd completely agree with him for once.

Forget about being optimistic. Optimism sucked.

"I liked working with him. It was kind of an apprentice thing," I explained.

"I see. Well, he did leave. I'm very sorry," Miss Crossley said. "So, can you be ready for the beach in about half an hour? Will Talbot is in need of a beach buddy."

I let out a deep breath, trying to release all the tension in my body.

It didn't work.

"Sure. Of course I can," I said. "I *love* the beach."

It's just that I'd love it a lot more if Hayden was assigned to another beach. Say, on Cape Cod. Just for a few days, just long enough for me to get my act together and fall back *out* of love with him.

I felt a hair color change coming on. Unfortunately I didn't think I had time to book an appointment at the Inn salon in the next ten minutes.

"Hey, you look great this morning," Hayden said when I showed up, trailing behind Will, who plowed straight ahead. He didn't even take off his sneakers before he sprinted into the water. He got his toes wet, then stopped, dropped to the sand, and started digging.

I glared at Hayden. "As opposed to other mornings?"

"What?" Hayden asked, looking confused. He apparently thought we'd made up; but since we hadn't talked since the night before, I didn't see how.

"Or as compared with Zoe," I said under my breath.

My attempt to be cool and pretend I wasn't hurt and that I was completely over him was failing. Badly.

"Is that the infamous fourth bathing suit?" Hayden asked.

I didn't answer him.

"Nice." He nodded as he stepped back to appraise me.

"Whatever," I said. "I think I'll focus on Will, thank you very much."

"Liza, swim with me!" Will yelled as he ran toward me.

"We're not swimming yet, but we can in a little bit," I said. I had it on good authority that Will had just eaten a late breakfast, so I wanted him to wait before we plunged into the ocean.

"No, now," he said.

"No, later," I said.

"You know what, buddy? Let's go on a shell hunt," Hayden offered.

I appreciated the gesture, but it was annoying as well. Did he think he needed to save me? I could handle Will on my own. "You're a lifeguard, not a nature lover," I said.

"I can't be both?" Hayden asked.

"Not when people are depending on you to save their life, no."

"There's nobody swimming," Hayden said.

"Maybe they heard you're the one on duty. Didn't feel like drifting out to sea while you searched for shells," I said.

He started to laugh. "Man, are you mad."

"Why wouldn't I be?" I replied.

Hayden was looking over my shoulder at something, or someone. "Caroline?" he said. I turned around.

"Your presence is requested in the dining room." She sounded as if she'd rather be anywhere else than talking to the two of us.

"What?" I asked.

"Yours, too," she told Hayden.

I was puzzled. "What's this all about?"

"I don't know what it's about, but Mr. Talbot wants to talk to you, over lunch," Caroline said in a bored tone.

"But ah—we're not dressed for the dining room," I protested. *And I don't want to go anywhere with Hayden!*

"Obviously. I can see that," Caroline said. "So Hayden, you go get cleaned up and changed as soon as Lindsay gets here to take over for you. Liza—you can go now."

"Who's going to replace—"

"*I* am, all right?" Caroline said, exasperated.

I backed away slowly, watching her attempt to play with Will. He took two giant handfuls of sand and threw them at her. Poor Caroline, I thought. And then, poor Will.

And then I thought—poor *me*. This could only be a good-bye lunch, if it was me, Hayden, and Mr. Talbot. He knew about the time we'd been on the deck—and he must have some new information on us. How embarrassing.

I bumped into Hayden on my way out of the dorm. I'd changed into a khaki skirt and a flowered blouse. My hair was tied up in a loose bun, sort of, with lots of tendrils falling out.

I expected Hayden to say something about my appearance, but he didn't. He just glanced at me and kept walking toward the Inn, not looking at me. It was like the two of us were bracing for a firing squad.

When we got to the dining room, Guess Who was working as both server and host.

"Right this way, please," Zoe said.

I hadn't even seen her since the infamous wedding.

This was exactly why Claire warned me about no hookups. The place was closing in on all sides.

"This isn't some weird Dr. Phil intervention to make us all talk, is it?" I asked her.

"What?" Zoe looked at me as if I were crazy.

"Never mind," I said as she led us to the Inn's best corner table, by the biggest window, with a clear view of the ocean. An older gentleman was sitting there—it was Mr. Talbot *Senior*. And across the table from him was . . .

"Grandpa?" I said.

"Drove down this morning." He stood up and I gave him a hug. "Surprise!"

"Yes, it's surprising, all right," I commented. "It's so nice to see you! Is Grandma here, too?"

"Yes, but she's visiting an old friend—she'll be by this afternoon."

"I've arranged for you to have the afternoon

off to spend with your grandparents," Mr. Talbot Senior said. "Miss Crossley's been notified."

"Wow. Thank you!" I said.

"You too, Hayden." Mr. Talbot nodded. "Enjoy the time off."

"Uh . . . thanks." Hayden opened his napkin and set it on his lap. I'm sure he was wondering, like I was, what the heck he was there for.

But then I vaguely remembered telling my grandfather about him, back when I was visiting him at the hospital. I sank down a little in my chair. I hoped my grandfather would be discreet, but then again, Hayden wouldn't be here now if I hadn't been indiscreet and blabbed about our possible relationship.

But you know what, I thought. If he was suffering and uncomfortable now, being here? That was too bad. He was the one who'd kissed *me* that night, before I left on the train to go home. He let me think we were in a relationship, and I'd only acted appropriately.

I wasn't the one being weird and hiding and going out with my former girlfriend just for appearance's sake. Not that I had a former girlfriend, but still.

"I understand you're feeling better, sir?" Hayden said to my grandfather.

"Oh, yes. Feeling just fine."

"Was something wrong?" Mr. Talbot asked.

"Just a touch of the flu, Bucko." My grandfather sipped his glass of lemonade. "Nothing serious."

"Grandpa," I said.

"It was a little warning from the old ticker, that's all," he explained. "A minor heart attack."

"I had one of those myself," Mr. Talbot said. "Maybe two or three."

I'm having one right now, I thought. *I don't know if I can sit here much longer.*

"So what have you two been up to?" my grandfather asked.

I shrugged. "Not much, really." Just sneaking away to closed beaches.

"Somehow I doubt that," he said. He turned to Hayden. "Are you treating her well?"

"Grandpa," I said through clenched teeth.

"You know, I'm always pleased when staff members become friends," Mr. Talbot said.

My grandfather chuckled. "Oh, Bucko, they're more than friends."

"Grandpa," I said again. If I gritted my teeth any more, sparks would fly off of them. *It's not like that—not anymore!* I wanted to scream. Why wasn't my grandmother there to rein him in?

"To young love." Grandpa raised his glass, just as Zoe came to the table to take our order.

"Excuse me," I said. "I'll be right back."

I pushed back my chair and practically sprinted for the women's room—except it wasn't that, it was a "ladies' lounge," with an elegant, antique sofa in an outer waiting room.

Once I was safely inside, I went to a sink and turned on the cold water, letting it run over my hands and wrists. I splashed my face and was searching for a towel to dry off when one was handed to me. I pressed it to my face, dried off, and looked up.

"We have to talk," Zoe said.

Chapter Twenty-two

"I ran into Claire this morning, in the hallway," Zoe went on. "Actually I think she was sitting out there waiting for me. I don't know how she found out what room I was in, but—"

"What are you talking about?" I asked.

"Here, in the Inn. You know I stayed with my sister last night—I mean, my whole family was here," she explained. She stepped up to the mirror and fixed her hair a little.

"Don't you need to get back to your tables?" I asked.

She shrugged. "Let them wait. The kitchen's running slow so far today, anyway." She leaned forward and touched up her lipstick. "So Claire told me about you and Hayden," she said casually.

This didn't seem like someone who was upset, but I wasn't completely sure.

"I had no idea you and Hayden were seriously involved. I'm really sorry you got the wrong impression last night. I'm still seeing Brandon, you know."

"That's what I thought," I said. "But then I see you and Hayden at the wedding . . . I mean, I saw you and Hayden together, and Brandon wasn't there . . . you have to admit that looked pretty bad."

"It was supposed to look good. To my parents," she said. "They love Hayden—or they love Hayden's family's money, anyway. When we broke up they were furious with me, all because Hayden's dad is some big-shot corporate guy and his family's so big and important in the community, and they thought it would be their 'in,' you know."

"Their 'in'?" I asked.

"They freak out about whether or not they're going to be accepted. We're sort of new in town. Anyway, I'm not seeing Hayden. My family doesn't approve of Brandon, that's all. We fought about it constantly. So I told them we were over, and I was back with Hayden."

"So is it like that on his end? Hayden's family wouldn't approve of me, either?"

Zoe shrugged. "What's there not to approve of?"

"I don't know. You tell me," I said.

"Well, we do come from kind of a snobby community, it's true. And our parents did want us to date, but that's not enough reason to actually stay together. Look, Claire said you guys argued, and I want to make it clear there was no reunion, or anything like that. We've been over since a year ago."

I wanted to believe Zoe, and for the most part I did, but a few things still didn't make sense. One, why did Hayden insist on being so secretive? And . . . "Then why did you kiss him?"

Zoe laughed. "I had a glass of champagne with my sister at the beginning of the reception—it went to my head. That's it. It didn't mean anything. Anyway, order the clam chowder and the lobster—it's the best stuff on the menu." Zoe opened the door and walked out of the ladies' room.

I fixed my hair for a second, then headed back to our table, where Hayden, Grandpa, and Mr. Talbot were all laughing about something. I opened my cloth napkin and smoothed it on my lap.

I couldn't believe Hayden hadn't taken the opportunity to bolt, without me there. But how could he? The owner of the Inn was dining with us. Neither one of us could leave.

"So," Grandpa said, turning to me. "What would you two like to do this afternoon?"

Hayden and I looked at each other across the table. I wondered if he was thinking what I was: *I'd like to get this lunch over with as soon as possible.*

Around 5:30 I was saying good-bye to my grandparents at the Inn's front entrance, by their car, when my grandmother said, "Is that little Carrie Farlane?"

I turned and saw Caroline walking up from the dorm. "Caroline, Grandma," I said. I tried to smile as I said it, so she wouldn't ask what was up.

"Caroline, how nice to see you!" my grandmother said as Caroline came closer.

"Hello, Mrs. McKenzie. Mr. McKenzie." She reached out her hand to shake theirs, but my grandparents insisted on hugging her. She looked embarrassed, but sort of happy, too.

"Wow. Look at the two of you, all grown up. I remember when you two ruled the roost," my grandfather said.

"We did what?" I asked.

"You were the dynamic duo. You were Lewis and she was Clark," my grandfather said.

I looked at Caroline and rolled my eyes. "Whatever, Grandpa."

"Enjoying your summer?" my grandmother asked Caroline.

"Definitely," Caroline said. "I mean, not everything is perfect, but—"

"You wouldn't want that," Grandpa interrupted as he walked around to the passenger side door. "Perfect is boring." He opened the door and slid into his seat, and I leaned in the open window and gave him a quick good-bye kiss on the cheek.

"We're on our way to meet friends, so we can't hang around. But it's so nice to see you, Caroline. Take care, Liza," my grandmother said as she got into the car. "Take care of each other, will you?" She waved out the window and called to us, "Have fun!"

I guessed I had never mentioned the fact that Caroline and I weren't exactly best pals anymore. We stood there waving at my grandparents, and I felt kind of awkward, as if we were kids again and they'd just dropped us off at the beach.

"How was lunch?" Caroline asked glumly as we watched them drive away.

"Okay. Weird, embarrassing. You know my grandfather, how he likes to joke around. So he joked about me and Hayden. Ha ha. So funny," I complained. I sat down on the wide steps. "I felt like it would never end."

"I don't know what you're so upset about," Caroline replied. She sat a few steps above me. "One, Hayden really likes you. Two, you had lunch with Mr. Talbot. *Senior*."

I decided to ignore the first part. "So?"

"So, I've been here two years and I've never had lunch with *any* of the Talbots," Caroline said.

"Oh. Well, it wasn't that fascinating," I said. "Confidentially and all."

"Still. It's not fair. You come here and in like two seconds you're part of the in crowd," Caroline complained.

"What? I am not," I said.

"Yes, you are," she said. She sounded really hurt about it, and I wondered if that was why she hadn't been glad to see me show up for the summer.

"Look. The only in crowd in my opinion is the one that you happen to be in. You know what I mean? It's your friends. It's something you create yourself," I said.

"Easy for you to say. It took me two months to make good friends last summer," Caroline said. "It was really hard. I mean, maybe if we both started here at the same time . . . it would have been easier, you know?"

"Yeah, it probably would have been. But you didn't make it easier on me when I showed up here," I reminded her.

"No. I guess not. I was so worried you were going to tell a bunch of embarrassing stories about me."

"Maybe I would have," I admitted. "If I knew any really *good* ones."

"Don't you?" Caroline asked.

"Not really. I mean, we were kids then," I said. "We did stupid things. It didn't matter — we had fun. Anyway, why do you care so much what everyone thinks?"

"Because! Don't you?" Caroline asked.

"Maybe at first," I admitted. "I definitely didn't like showing up and feeling like an outsider. But then, I knew my way around town, and I was working pretty hard so I didn't have time to worry about it, and I got to be friends with Claire, and Josh —"

"And Hayden —"

"And I kind of stopped worrying about it," I said. "But earlier, you were saying . . . Hayden really likes me?"

"Liza, you sound like when we were twelve," Caroline laughed. "You wondered all the time whether that boy at Sally's coffee shop liked you."

"Well, yeah, didn't *you*?"

"No," Caroline said in a haughty tone. "I *knew* he liked me."

"And you were going to ask him out—but then I was going to ask him out first—and then we saw him making out with that girl—"

We both burst out laughing.

"Oh my God, I was so crushed," Caroline said. "Totally devastated. I wrote about ten pages in my journal that night. Which reminds me, I have got to burn that thing." She smiled and stretched her legs out on the step. "So . . . how come we were so sure of everything back then?"

"Yeah, that's kind of funny. I don't know," I said.

There was a loud beeping sound and I pulled the pager out of my pocket. "Do you think Miss Crossley was standing up there in her office, waiting for my grandparents to drive off?" I asked Caroline.

"I wouldn't put it past her," Caroline said under her breath. We started to laugh, and then Caroline said, "*Don't* tell her I said that. Promise me."

"I wouldn't," I assured her. "See you later."

I realized I'd never really gotten an answer to my question, as to whether Caroline thought Hayden was still interested in me. But it didn't matter, really. At the moment I was just glad that we'd had at least one good conversation, and I wasn't totally crazy. We had been really good friends once. Maybe we wouldn't be again, but we didn't have to be enemies, either. I should thank my grandparents, probably.

I went up to Miss Crossley's office and poked my head into her office. "You rang?" I asked. "Do you need me?"

"Yes, uh, we—wait a second, Liza." She shuffled some papers on her desk. "We've just had word from Mr. Wallace. He's changed his mind and is heading back to the Inn, so I'd like you to go on the shuttle with Hayden to the train station. I think he'd appreciate if you welcomed him back," Miss Crossley said.

"But . . . can't Hayden do that by himself?"
I asked.

"You're the one he has a connection with,
since you worked as his assistant. It would be
best if you went too. Meet Hayden by the shuttle at 6:30, all right?"

*Miss Crossley? I've been really, really flexible.
For days and weeks now. I've done everything you
asked,* I wanted to say. *But please don't make me do
this, because I'm not ready to see Hayden and spend
time alone with him yet.*

"Okay, fine," I said.

Fortunately we had guests to bring to the train,
so Hayden and I didn't have to be alone—
or talk—during the ride into town. We dropped
them off, then waited for the train from Boston
to arrive. I paced around the platform, trying to
keep my distance, while Hayden leaned against
the van looking bored.

Why did Miss Crossley do this to us?
Couldn't one person easily handle this task?

When the train showed up, I didn't see C. Q.

anywhere. I looked up and down the platform, watching every train door for a glimpse of him. But nobody appeared.

"Do you think he missed the train?" I asked as I walked back to Hayden. It was pulling away from the station. "Or maybe he fell asleep and missed the announcement for this stop?"

"What are you saying? He wasn't on the train?" Hayden asked.

Had he fallen asleep standing there? "Do you *see* him?" I asked.

"No, I guess not." Hayden tossed the set of keys into the air and caught them. "Oh, well. I'm not going to worry about it, I'm sure he'll call. Let's head back. Unless you want to grab an ice cream first?"

"Aren't you worried at all?" I asked as I climbed into the van through the sliding door.

Hayden turned around from the front seat, a puzzled expression on his face. "Aren't you going to sit up here?"

"No, I hadn't planned on it," I said.

"Well, it just feels weird, like I'm a taxi driver."

"Well. Aren't you?"

Hayden narrowed his eyes at me. "You know, your grandfather is a lot nicer than you are."

"Let's not get into discussing the topic of nice. You're the one who went on a date with someone else without even warning me."

"It wasn't a date," Hayden said as he started the van.

"Whatever. Let's get back to the Inn and tell Miss Crossley her favorite guest isn't checking back in." I scrunched down in my seat and tried to ignore the fact that even the tiniest glimpse of Hayden, from the backseat, was attractive.

"What are we doing here?"

Hayden parked the van outside the closed, dilapidated hotel. He got out of the van and walked around to open the sliding door. "I wanted to stop someplace private on the way back—somewhere we could be alone and talk."

"We could have been alone at the train station. We *were* alone. So why not then?" I asked.

"Just . . . come on. Walk on the beach with me," Hayden urged. He held out his hand.

This isn't fair, I thought as I got out of the shuttle, on my own. *Revisiting the scene of a crime of passion. Or just . . . the scene of passion.*

"This doesn't mean anything. That I'm willing to walk on the beach with you," I said.

"Okay, fine, it doesn't mean anything," Hayden said. "You're just here for the sea air and exercise."

"Don't make fun of me," I said, but I was trying not to smile.

"I'd never," Hayden said.

We walked through the broken-down gate on the side of the hotel that led to the beach.

My eyes widened as I saw dozens of flowers strewn all over the sand. I wandered closer, stepping over a ring of white, pink, yellow, and red roses, mixed in with daisies and lilies. "How did these—where did you get all these?" I asked.

"One was a bouquet I stole from the front desk. Caroline turned her back."

"She should know not to do that when you're around," I said, and Hayden grinned.

"The rest I borrowed from the Inn's flower garden," Hayden said. "It was overflowing— I doubt anyone will notice. And before you say anything, it's not that I wouldn't buy flowers for you, but I really didn't have the opportunity—"

"No, it's okay. It's really nice," I told him.

I looked around and noticed a couple of the Inn's deluxe beach towels, folded and sitting atop a cooler.

"In case we feel like swimming. And I brought some mineral water and some shrimp cocktail because I heard you really like that," Hayden said.

And I was so about to get sucked in by the love undertow, which was quickly turning into a riptide. I dug my heels into the sand to stop myself.

"No, you're not doing this again," I said.

"What?" Hayden asked. "Doing what?"

"You have no problem being with me out—out here," I said. "If no one's around, then that's fine. You're wonderfully sweet and everything. But then in public, you have to either be single, or with Zoe, or—I don't know. But I'm not okay with the whole Privacy Please thing."

"So you're into the voyeur thing, then," Hayden said.

"Not funny," I said.

"Look, I came here because I wanted us to be alone. I want to spend time with you. Just you. I don't want people watching us, or commenting, or—"

"Or knowing about us," I said. "I don't know why, I really don't. But I've never been one to hide before. And I'm not going to be now."

"But don't you think it's kind of fun? Kind of, I don't know. Exciting. To have a secret?"

"I'm not happy being your secret," I said. "I thought I kind of made that clear, but apparently not."

"You're not being fair," Hayden said. "I'm trying to make it up to you. What do you think, do you think all this stuff happened by accident? I arranged it all. I convinced Miss Crossley. You were on the beach with Will because of me, you went on the shuttle tonight because of me—"

"So what? That doesn't mean anything." It did, sort of, but I wasn't ready to give him credit for that. "Let's go," I said.

"Liza. Come on," he said.

This was killing me, but I had to do it. I walked over to the van and opened the passenger door. "Let's go."

Chapter Twenty-three

I walked out onto the Inn porch the next morning around eleven and stopped dead in my tracks. "Where did you come from?"

"Nantucket," C. Q. Wallace said. His feet were up on the railing, and he had a notebook in his lap.

"Really?" I laughed. "No—I mean . . . we went to pick you up last night, and you weren't there."

"You came to pick me up in Nantucket? How thoughtful."

"Yeah, well, I wanted to take a road trip," I joked. "No, we went to the train station to get you."

"Interesting. I wasn't coming on the train," he said.

"You never called to say that you were?" I asked.

He shook his head.

So Hayden had fabricated that whole scenario, like he said. And I was kind of impressed. He had persuaded Miss Crossley to let me go on an errand that even she knew wasn't real.

"I rented a car and drove down," C. Q. explained. "Got in this morning. And now that I have wheels, I'll be able to get my own pens from now on."

"Great," I murmured, wondering if I'd underestimated Hayden.

"Anyway. I assume Miss Crossley told you the drill? Can you type some of this stuff up for me?"

"She actually didn't tell me, but I'm not in the middle of anything else, so sure," I said. I figured Miss Crossley must be ill, since it was so late in the day and I hadn't yet been summoned. "But if you wrote it in Nantucket, how accurate can it be about this place?"

"Liza, it's a funny thing. But sometimes you need to leave a place in order to write about it. It's a matter of perspective." He handed me a pad of legal paper. "If you can type this new material up, I can e-mail it to my editor this afternoon and have her insert it into the manuscript."

"Okay," I said. "I guess." The whole process sounded weird and sort of unprofessional to me, but I guessed someone who wrote best sellers knew more than I did.

Dear Liza, I typed.

"Wait a second," I said. "Is this where my character gets really important to the plot?"

"Just type it," he said.

I stared at the piece of paper. It was familiar handwriting, but I didn't think it was his. "This doesn't look like your handwriting."

"I wrote it when I was driving."

"You write and drive? That is so wrong."

"Just type," he said again.

I'm sorry. I realize what you mean about secrets. And you're right—I have been a phony. I need to fix that. Hayden.

"Is this all you have?" I asked. "Did you write this?"

"Please. I think I have a little more literary style than that, don't you?"

I smiled and gazed at the ocean. It was a beautiful day; the sun was sparkling on the water and a light breeze blew my hair back from my face. "Can you give me like five minutes?" I asked.

"I suppose," he sighed. "But seriously, after this, I do have something for you to type."

"I'll be right back." I sprinted down the boardwalk. As angry as I still was with Hayden, I wanted to see him and talk to him. He could apologize a few more times and explain what it was all about. Maybe I'd forgive him this time. I could see he really was trying now.

But when I got to the beach, Hayden was nowhere in sight. Lindsay was sitting on top of the lifeguard chair. I waved to her. "Is Hayden around?" I asked, forgetting my wounded pride for a second.

"He's gone for a few days," Lindsay said. "He went home."

"Home?" That seemed a little strange. I hoped nothing was wrong. "When is he coming back, do you know?"

"Saturday, I think," Lindsay said.

"Oh. Okay. Thanks!"

I walked back up to the Inn, wondering if there was a way to reach Hayden while he was home, or if I should bother. He'd made such a nice gesture the night before, and now this note . . .

But would it change anything?

"Got the tray?" Daunte teased me as I walked past him into the dining room on Saturday. We were hosting another wedding at the Inn.

"Yes, I have it," I said, rolling my eyes.

"You sure?"

"I'm sure." I shifted the tray of raspberry sorbet dishes in my arms. Every single one of my coworkers had been giving me a hard time about the way I'd dropped my tray the week before.

I flashed back to the last wedding. With any luck, this event wouldn't be nearly as disastrous, or as painful.

Then I saw Hayden get up onstage, next to the DJ. I didn't even know he'd come back yet. What was he doing? Was he going to sing? Was this a karaoke wedding?

"Excuse me, everyone. Could I have your

attention please? I'd like to make a toast."

"Richard," I said, pulling his best friend aside. "He's not a guest at this wedding too, is he?"

"No, he doesn't know them at all." Richard smiled at me. "Don't worry, okay?"

What was Hayden doing? Now they were hiring the Inn to even take care of their toasts? What *wouldn't* these people spend money on?

"My name is Hayden, and normally I'd just park your cars, but today I have a special announcement. But if this takes too long or is too boring and you need your car, just raise your hand."

A few people in the audience laughed, while Hayden unfolded a crumpled piece of paper and cleared his throat. "Bear with me a second here. Okay." He looked at the crowd, but didn't seem to notice where I was standing. "I don't really know Maisie and Jacob, but, uh, I do know something about, uh, love," he said.

Just to be on the safe side, I set the tray of sorbet on the table closest to me.

"The thing about love is that you can't predict it," Hayden went on. "You can't plan it.

It's like the weather."

Like the weather? I thought. *Doesn't the weather change really frequently? Some days love is warm, some days it's cold* . . . Where was he going with this? And why?

Claire came up beside me. "I don't know what he's doing, but I think it's going to be good," she whispered.

Josh stood behind her, his chin resting on her shoulder. "Or really, really awful," he said.

"Great," I muttered.

"Sorry, I can't read his—my handwriting." Hayden seemed to be squinting at the tiny piece of paper. "The person we love is the one we follow. The one who tells us how to be in the world, and lets us know whether we're doing the right thing or not. They're our bellwether," Hayden went on.

"Barometer!" someone in the crowd yelled out.

"Barometer," Hayden said, nodding. "That makes sense." He looked up at everyone. "You've got to check out the big barometer in the lobby, if you haven't already. Antique. Really cool." He took a deep breath and rubbed his neck, looking uncomfortable. "Anyway. True love can't be measured by a barometer, but if it could be . . ." He squinted at the paper again, then crumpled it into a ball and shoved it in his pocket. "Oh, what the heck. Liza? I'm sorry I've been such a jerk. I want everyone here—especially you—to know that . . . well, I really love you. Now just dance with me, okay?"

He handed the microphone back to the DJ and hopped off the stage. On his way over to me, as the music started, he took his key to the valet key cabinet and handed it to Miss Crossley. Before he could take another step, I rushed toward him, and he caught me in his arms.

I think maybe a couple of people were clapping. Maybe everybody was clapping. But I didn't hear them or the music, I was so happy.

We danced for a minute, and then I said, "Why isn't anyone else dancing? It's not *our* wedding. I feel like we're onstage. Everyone's watching us."

"See? I told you privacy wasn't all bad—"

"But it's okay," I said.

"Okay. Yeah, it is," Hayden said, smoothing my hair. "But still. You want to get out of here?" he whispered in my ear.

"Do I ever," I said. "But I've got this tray of melting sorbet—"

"Got it," Hayden said. He grabbed the tray off the table where I'd left it and we quickly handed out dishes. Then we headed for the exit, and as we were walking out, C. Q. Wallace was lingering near the open doorway. "C. Q. helped me with the speech," Hayden explained.

"You mangled it, but oh well," C. Q. commented with a smile. "Now where's that wedding cake?" He moved past us into the dining room.

Hayden and I laughed and ran out onto the porch together, holding hands. I knew exactly where we were heading.

"You know, you could sell that piece of paper on eBay," I told him as I hopped off the boardwalk. I slipped off my shoes and left them in the sand. "Except that I'm not going to let you, because I'm going to save it."

"So how have you been?" Hayden asked as

we walked toward the water.

"Fine. Bored. You?" I asked. "How was the visit at home?"

"We got some stuff sorted out. And I told them all about you."

"You didn't."

"I did. They'll be here next week to visit," Hayden said. "You can try to talk Grace out of her gothness."

"What? No way. I want her to like me," I said.

We stopped at the water's edge. We were both still wearing our catering uniforms. "So," Hayden said.

"So."

"Same as usual?" he asked.

"With a twist," I said. I reached up and put my arms around his neck, pulling him closer for a kiss.

Then, when he was really getting into it, I broke away and sprinted into the water.

"Hey! No fair!" He rushed in after me, diving under a big wave that was about to break. Hayden came up for air and dove again, this time tugging at my ankle. I held my breath and went underwater, too, and just as I did, my pager started to buzz. Underwater. Completely submerged. I pulled it out of my pocket to show Hayden, and he smiled, little air bubbles coming out of his mouth.

Miss Crossley wouldn't believe me even if I told her the truth about where I'd been when she paged me. So I wouldn't bother to tell her. Besides, it had to stop beeping soon. Right?

Don't miss these other great reads from Catherine Clark!

Maine Squeeze

Colleen usually thinks that living on a tiny island off the coast of Maine is boring. But this summer she has a new job, a great boyfriend, and a house with no parents—perfect! That is, until last summer's boyfriend shows up, and Colleen's small island gets a lot smaller.

The Alison Rules

Alison does her best to keep things under control—if you follow the rules, you won't get hurt. But rules are meant to be broken, and when funny, charming Patrick moves to town, things start to change for Alison, and all her unbreakable rules are put to the test.

Icing on the Lake

New Year's Resolutions by Kirsten

1. Survive the month at my sister's house. Survive my 3-year-old nephew and crazy sister.

2. Learn to ice skate better. Or not fall down. Or just get a cuter skating outfit.

3. Find hockey-playing, winter-loving hottie. And invite him to the weekend cabin trip.

Oh sure, no problem.